SALT WATER

SALT WATER

and other stories

by

BARBARA WILSON

ALL CHARACTERS IN THIS BOOK ARE FICTITIOUS. ANY RESEMBLANCE TO REAL INDIVIDUALS, EITHER LIVING OR DEAD, IS STRICTLY COINCIDENTAL.

COVER PHOTOGRAPH BY CHRISTOPHER HARRITY.

MANUFACTURED IN THE UNITED STATES OF AMERICA.

THIS TRADE PAPERBACK ORIGINAL IS PUBLISHED BY ALYSON PUBLICATIONS INC.,
P.O. BOX 4371, LOS ANGELES, CALIFORNIA 90078-4371.
DISTRIBUTION IN THE UNITED KINGDOM BY TURNAROUND PUBLISHER SERVICES LTD.,
UNIT 3, OLYMPIA TRADING ESTATE, COBURG ROAD, WOOD GREEN,
LONDON N22 6TZ, ENGLAND.

FIRST EDITION: JANUARY 1999

99 00 01 02 03 a 10 9 8 7 6 5 4 3 2 1

ISBN 1-55583-486-8

LIBRARY OF CONGRESS CATALOGING-IN-PUBLICATION DATA

WILSON, BARBARA, 1950–

SALT WATER AND OTHER STORIES / BY BARBARA WILSON. — 1ST ED.

CONTENTS: SALT WATER—WE DIDN'T SEE IT—IS THIS ENOUGH FOR YOU?—I MET A DOG IN THE PYRENEES—ARCHEOLOGY—WOOD—THE WOMAN WHO MARRIED HER SON'S WIFE—SUIT OF LEATHER—SILKIE.

ISBN 1-55583-486-6

1. LESBIANS—SOCIAL LIFE AND CUSTOMS—FICTION. I. TITLE.

PS3573.I45678S25 1999
813'.54—DC21 98-46380 CIP

CREDITS

•AN EXCERPT FROM "SALT WATER" FIRST APPEARED IN *HOT TICKET,* EDITED BY LINNEA DUE (ALYSON BOOKS, 1997).

•"WE DIDN'T SEE IT" FIRST APPEARED IN *LESBIAN LOVE STORIES I,* EDITED BY IRENE ZAHAVA (CROSSING PRESS, 1989).

•"IS THIS ENOUGH FOR YOU?" FIRST APPEARED IN *LESBIAN LOVE STORIES II,* EDITED BY IRENE ZAHAVA (CROSSING PRESS, 1991)

•"I MET A DOG IN THE PYRENEES" FIRST APPEARED IN *ZYZZYVA, 39*, SPRING, 1994.

•"WOOD" FIRST APPEARED IN *LOVE SHOOK MY HEART: LESBIAN LOVE STORIES,* EDITED BY IRENE ZAHAVA (ALYSON BOOKS, 1998).

•"THE WOMAN WHO MARRIED HER SON'S WIFE" FIRST APPEARED IN *QUEER VIEW MIRROR II,* EDITED BY JAMES C. JOHNSTONE AND KAREN X. TULCHINSKY (ARSENAL PULP PRESS, 1997).

•"SUIT OF LEATHER" FIRST APPEARED IN *PILLOW TALK,* EDITED BY LESLÉA NEWMAN (ALYSON BOOKS, 1998).

Contents

Part One

Salt Water

I. Woman Before an Open Window

She's in one of those photo albums that I rarely open anymore. Plain blue vinyl cover; stick-on pages going yellow at the corners. Why would I think to open it? It's full of photographs of a foreign place, of a woman I lost contact with long ago.

But if I opened it, I would find her on an island off the coast of Sweden. The wind is blowing her fine brown-gold hair as she sits on a bench at the harbor. Our bikes are parked nearby, my old straw hat dangling off my handlebars. We're waiting for the ferry to the mainland or perhaps another island where we plan to take a ride. There are several photos like that in this album, of us waiting for a ferry; I must have taken them to pass the time and gotten passers-by to snap a shot or two of both of us. I'm smaller than she is, wearing glasses, my short blond hair ruffling in the breeze. We both look brown, cheerful, very young, though we were in our early 30s. Other photos show her in her garden, all rocks and tiles and ceramic pots, the pink roses and red and purple hollyhocks climbing up the side of her wooden yellow house. There are a few of her on the rocks where we used to sunbathe by the two pools at the edge of the island. She's never fully clothed in the garden or by the sea. She didn't like my taking pictures, I remember now. Perhaps that's why she's frowning, just slightly, but impatiently.

Most of the photos are from the first time I visited her, one week in June, more than ten years ago. A few are from the following summer, when I stayed on the island much of the month of August. I hardly dared take any then. I didn't want her to think I was looking at her too intently.

None of my friends ever knew her, and few of them would remember if I said her name now. Monika Diechmann. "One of those straight women you were always fantasizing about?" Beth might tease, amused and sure in our love that those days are long behind me. Or Evie might say vaguely, "Wasn't she *German* or something?"

The photo album isn't where I would look if I wanted to remember her. I would probably pull out the packet of thin square blue envelopes, 12 in all, with a postcard of a whitewashed Greek village tucked on top. I might trace the lines of her script to try to recall what was important to her to tell me. I suppose I would find a lot of words about solitude and loneliness, about her longing for a full-time, absorbing creative life. Fingering the letters might give me back that sense of possibility and joy I had every time I found one in my letterbox; it might bring back her precise and considered speech. I might hear her say again, "Oh, Anne, how can I make you understand?"

If I really wanted to see her again, though, I would dig through the many boxes in the studio and find my sketchbooks from those two Swedish summers, when I first began life drawing. She would not be posing—she had her own work to do—but standing before an open window, the curtains white, diaphanous, blowing into the room, the sea beyond, roaring silently on the page. I think I would not be ashamed of the drawings, even though they were often rough and crude (the foreshortening a struggle then, the angle of her thin neck and narrow shoulders always a problem. I never captured her exactly.)

If I could find that box of sketches underneath everything that has piled up since, I would probably also find the watercolors that I did, single sheets placed carefully in a portfolio. I once planned to have them framed, for I thought them fresh and lovely. I wonder if I still would, or if I would be indifferent, would shrug them off the way we do so many things we loved once, as faulty and imperfect.

It seems longer ago than ten years that I first met Monika. At the time I was finishing up a six months' stay in Norway, where a Fulbright had given me the chance to take a semester off from my position teaching art history at a small college in Minnesota. A few years before, I'd finished my dissertation on a circle of Norwegian women painters active in the second half of the 19th century. Now I was narrowing my research to study two of the most prominent of the circle, Harriet Backer and Kitty Kielland. In the large galleries of Oslo and Bergen and Stavanger, and in smaller provincial museums and private collections, I had looked long and hard at all the paintings of theirs I could find, and had read what I could about them and about the feminist movement in Norway at the turn of the century. I was preparing to write a monograph when I returned home, and perhaps some less academic articles.

I was an ambitious but not driven 32-year-old, full of great enthusiasm for my subject. I'd been teaching for about five years at my college and was hoping to get tenure soon, though most of my work had been on women's art, and the school was rather conservative. I was closeted of course, but not particularly miserable about it. I lived alone, and though nothing lasting had yet worked out for me, I was sure it would. In general things had worked out for me. Without thinking much about it, I would probably have considered myself happy and, except for not being able to talk about my personal life with most of my colleagues or family, quite well-adjusted and socially at ease. I was still pleased about having a Ph.D. and having some connection to the world of ideas and culture. I had come from a small town in Minnesota where people did not get above themselves, at least not very far, without being punished, either by God or gossip, so I was used to being modest about my accomplishments, which did not prevent me from being secretly proud.

Oslo, then, in early June, a cool bright summer evening full of delicacy and possibility. An acquaintance called Astrid, another art professor, had picked me up and was taking me to the opening of a show of contemporary Swedish women artists. Imposing as usual in a handwoven tunic and heavy wooden beads, Astrid lectured me until we got there on women's liberation and the female artist, a subject she had recently discovered. The gallery was packed with tall Scandinavians imbibing freely. The art was the usual mix, for that time, the early '80s, and place, of styles and subjects. A few sentimental figurative paintings of mothers and children, some nudes of men, meant to shock, a great number of murky and jarring abstracts, and plenty of wall hangings and sculpture constructions making use of Swedish craft techniques. A few pieces had an obvious, even mythological female sensibility, such as the painting of a woman giving birth to the planet earth. Most, however, were reflections of current preoccupations with medium as opposed to subject matter. There was something huge and paint-slathered and industrial and thick and rope-twined and plastered about almost everything there.

There was only one artist, one set of paintings that drew me. Each of the six canvases was small compared to the rest of the exhibit, and each had the dominating image of a rock or a rocky island in the center of a stained color field that suggested the unsettling pale blue of sky or water, but that had no horizon. Around the rock, at the edges of the canvases, marched and spun meticulously rendered seashells and pebbles. The effect was one of lightness but not playfulness, a little vertiginous and very solitary.

I asked Astrid about the painter, whose name I could see was Monika Diechmann.

"She's not really Swedish, you know," Astrid whispered. "Some of the others seem to think she shouldn't be in the show. Her mother's Swedish, and she spends her summers in Sweden, on some island off the coast near Göteborg, but she's really German, and most of the year she lives in Cologne."

I went over to the woman Astrid pointed out. She had a perfectly oval face with a broad brow, on a fragile, even spindly neck. Her brown-gold hair was pulled back into a knot, and she was wearing thin gold hoops. Her eyes were large and light green, slightly protuberant with thin bluish lids. She had on some lipstick and was wearing a cream knit pullover that showed a naked brown shoulder. If it had not been for her tan, which was quite dark, she might have looked like a Madonna from a Northern Renaissance painting.

I'd learned Norwegian to pursue my research, but was still better at reading than speaking, for almost everyone I worked with in Norway spoke perfect English. I stumbled even saying something simple to her, namely that I found her work interesting, and she answered me, in a clear, steady voice, in English. Her accent was German.

"And what interests you?"

"The translucency. Everything around the island shimmers with light. The seashells look as if they have tiny bulbs inside them."

Afterward, when Astrid asked me what we'd talked about, I told her that Monika had said, "Thank you for not asking what it all means."

We had talked instead about technique and had quickly come to an agreement that we did not care much for anyone else's art here but hers. "And are you an artist yourself?" she asked me.

"No, an art historian. A professor." I told her about Harriet Backer and Kitty Kielland and the research I had done and was doing on the circle of women painters in Norway a hundred years ago.

I was explaining to her how thrilling it had been for me to discover the existence of this group and to see the ways in which women had helped each other in the earlier wave of the feminist movement, when Monika interrupted, "And weren't there any women who were not part of this circle?" She had a quizzical, not unfriendly look.

"Yes, there was one. At least one. Oda Krohg. She doesn't fit into my research very well. She was not a spinster who saw art as the only alternative to being a governess. She was not quite respectable. She married young and had two children, then began to study painting with Christian Krohg, the bohemian painter and novelist. She divorced her first husband and married Krohg, and had two more children. She was the girl in the bad-boy gang of the 1880s."

"Why don't you write about her?"

"Because I'm interested in the larger picture, not the anomaly."

Monika's broad brow knitted, as if she were trying to understand. "But the important thing is, do you like her paintings?"

"I like her paintings almost more than anyone's," I admitted.

"That's very strange then, that you only write about Harriet Backer and Kitty Kielland."

"I like their paintings too," I said, but Monika turned away. She surveyed the room, which had gotten even more stuffy and crowded, and she waved her hand at the walls. "I wonder," she said, "in a hundred years, if this will be called a circle? If I will be mentioned as part of a circle of Swedish women painters?"

"It's easier for art historians to see painters in groups," I said. "Those outside the groups sometimes don't get seen."

"I want to be seen. And yet I feel I have nothing in common with them," she said, fixing those large light eyes on me. They were the color of just-peeled green grapes, and that shape too, underneath the thin eyelids. She was so delicate that it seemed she might break, but when I looked at her hands I saw they were long-fingered and strong. I found myself wanting to take hold of one of them. "Not as a woman, not as a painter," Monika said, almost wistfully, looking around.

"Oh, I hate that kind of opportunistic person," Astrid said afterwards, dropping me off at my rented room. "Doesn't want to call herself a feminist, hardly even a woman, yet is perfectly happy to be asked to exhibit in a show called Swedish Women Painters. I mean, she's not even really Swedish!"

"She lives there three months of every year," I protested. "On that island. She said I could come visit her next week. Before I leave for home."

"She asked you to come stay?" Astrid stared. "Are you sure you didn't misunderstand? You only talked a few minutes. And all the Swedes have been complaining how unfriendly she is."

Silently I held out my hand. In it was a tiny slip of paper, and it said, in tiny letters: "Monika Diechmann. Take the train to Göteborg. Walk to the bus station and take the bus to the ferry dock at R. Take the ferry to A. Anyone can tell you my address."

The island of A. was the last stop of a ferry that traveled through an archipelago of small stony islands. A. seemed, as we approached it, to rise straight out of the sea, a pyramid of rock with pastel houses scattered up and down its slopes and red boat sheds clustered around the natural harbor. It was midafternoon, all sparkle and light, the scent of diesel oil, fish, and the ocean mixed together in the sunshine. I stepped over fishing nets on the dock and avoided children and dogs. As a stranger I found it all looked festive and yet unwelcoming, the way a new place can seem to be. I had been traveling, by train, bus, and ferry, since 6 this morning.

I had written a card to Monika to tell her the day and approximate time I'd be arriving, but she wasn't there to greet me at the dock. I asked a fisherman working on his boat where I might find her. He jerked his head up the hill, without saying anything, and I began to walk along the dock, past a small store and a line of red-painted boat sheds, and then up the only street I could see, a narrow winding path paved with large stones and occasional steps. From this path other smaller paths led off, to painted wooden cottages, some rather shabby, some bowered by climbing roses and clematis, with cats in the windows and weather vanes on the roofs. I asked the few people I met on the path about Monika's house and they always pointed up, and higher.

What if she hadn't been serious about the visit? What if she'd forgotten all about my coming? What if the postcard I'd sent hadn't gotten here? What if she wasn't expecting me, didn't want me? What if she didn't live alone or had a lover here?

I had told my landlady in Oslo so gaily that I was going off to Sweden for a week. I had told everyone I knew. It had made me feel happy and special and as if something amazing were about to happen. I had held in my mind the picture of the dancing seashells around the mysterious rock and the picture of those light green eyes in the brown face.

There was one last house, high up on the hill, with an unhampered view of the sea. It was yellow and had been newly painted. There were small-paned windows, red shutters, a garden in back, protected by a dry stone wall with plants growing over it and in the crevices. I walked the last steps up the path, and up the stairs of the red porch with its potted geraniums. Knocked on the door. I could smell the ocean, the salt of it, in every breath I took. There was no answer, and unsure of what else to do, I sat down on the porch and after a moment, fell into a doze.

"Oh, there you are," she said, waking me up, coming around the side of the house, pulling on a shirt over her bikini bottom. "I was working in the garden."

She pressed her body quickly close to mine and kissed my cheek. She smelled of nut oil and dirt. I felt her breasts, careless, under the open shirt.

"Did you get my card?" I said.

"Oh, yes. How amazing that you actually came!" A sudden shyness seemed to come over her. "I don't have many visitors. None, in fact."

I still dream sometimes about the house that Monika lived in, and when I dream, it's always summer, always June. I still wake wishing I lived there, in that house that managed to be large and light and high on a stone hill, and yet secretive and hidden too, surrounded by flowers and dry stone walls, wound through with cubbyholes and crannies. Downstairs it was old-fashioned, with heavy furniture and objects left from earlier generations. There was a sunporch with a writing secretary piled with bills and letters, two pantries, one of which had been remodeled into a bathroom, and a dark, rather dingy kitchen, which had only a two-burner stove and a small refrigerator. There was a dining room, its carved table also piled with papers and boxes and laundry to be sorted and, through etched glass doors, a large parlor, with crumbling leather chairs and horse-hair settee, a tall clock with a painted, unmoving face, a piano that was out of tune, worn thick red carpets, and shelves of leather-bound books and old music scores and literary journals. There was a large tile stove, its tiles decorated in bright folk fashion, like something you might see in a painting by Carl Larsson, but sadly stained with smoke. It had been years since the house had been in frequent use. Most of the journals, brown-edged, were from the '50s, when Monika's uncle had lived here for a time, she explained. "He was running from the world," she said. "He was a book critic who wanted to write a novel and never did."

Upstairs, however, all was light and bare. In the small room Monika showed me to, there was only a single wooden bed painted French blue, with a yellow-striped comforter. A painted table and a brass lamp. A straight-backed chair. No closet or dresser, but an old-fashioned washbasin and pitcher, set under a window that faced the sea. When Monika opened the shutters, I had a view of other islands of the archipelago and could hear the waves crashing below on the rocks. There were two other small rooms like it upstairs, one of which Monika slept in, but they were above the garden and faced the harbor from which I'd climbed. Red and purple hollyhocks had climbed up nearly to the second floor. When I looked down I saw a white wrought iron table and chairs in the midst of roses, geraniums, and stock. The largest room, once a bedroom, had been turned into a studio, which Monika called her atelier. Like my room, it fronted the sea, and its windows, tall and narrow, small-paned, in a row, took up most of one wall. The windows were slightly open, and the strong fresh ocean breeze came in and blew the long curtains, of some thin ivory material, perhaps chiffon, in streamers toward us.

"I work here every morning," said Monika. "Sometimes all day."

The smell of oils and turpentine mixed with the warm ocean breeze; there were two old walnut tables covered with paints and sketches and shells and stones. A chair or two, and a bookcase haphazardly filled with battered and interesting art books in several languages. Large canvases everywhere, too much to take in all at once.

Monika stood before the open window, looking out to sea, breathing deep, and her darkly tanned body, still unself-consciously half-nude, made a shape, cut out of shadow, in front of the light.

Then she turned and smiled at me. "Do you think you could be happy here?"

The island did not have beaches, sandy or otherwise. The edges ran for the most part straight down to the sea, except at the natural harbor, which was protected by a breakwater. This harbor was the focal point of the small community; it had the store and post office and one café; it was where the foot ferry arrived and departed, and where the small fishing boats jostled uneasily with the sailboats and cruisers of the summer people and visitors.

No one swam at the harbor. In fact you couldn't swim off the island at all; the rocks were too steep and sharp and the currents too unreliable. Parents took their children to one end of the island, where the rocks sloped in into a shallow inner pool and where someone had constructed a slide. The other place to take a dip wasn't far from Monika's house, though it was a bit of a scramble down over the hill and over a series of vertically angled slabs of smooth dark rock. Because it was hard to get to, it was not much frequented, and certainly not by many of the summer visitors or children. However, it was one of the nearest places on the island to the sea, and the area had flat dark rocks all around it, perfect for sunbathing. As I've said, you couldn't actually swim in the sea. There were, instead, two pools. One was shaped like a bottle or a vase. It had a channel carved by the waves which led to a pool, filled with green cold water, that was about shoulder high. Even though it wasn't terribly deep it would have been impossible to get in or out of without the help of a ladder, which had been bolted to the side of one of the smooth rock slabs. The other pool was much shallower and lay even closer to the water and was more subject to its movements. For the larger pool was protected by its channel from the roughest of the waves.

This was not true of the shallower pool, although at first I found it the quieter, warmer, more restful place to be. I had, the first day I went to the ocean with Monika, lowered myself down by the ladder into the vase-shaped pool and had been shocked by its coldness, its tartness. I hesitated and then plunged: Immediately there was a fresh stinging at my eyes and nose and when I surfaced I had the taste of salt adhering to the corners of my mouth.

I had never swum in salt water before.

I did not find it refreshing. I felt as if my heart had stopped from the cold plunge and from the harsh briny taste of the sea. I had nothing to compare it to, for I had only swum in lakes and ponds before, and they were freshwater, though often muddy and full of bugs.

I got out immediately, gasping. Although the air was warm, my body had goose bumps and even looked slightly bluish. As my skin dried, a faint white powder remained on the surface, and when I tasted it, it was salty. Of course the sea is salt, you learn that as a child, but a book fact is different than a physical one.

Monika had plunged in after me and was still there, splashing and standing up and and swimming small strokes around the rim of the pool. Her brown head poked out, seal-like, and she kept her face upturned and laughed at me. "Too cold? No, it's just right. It's *perfect.*" She had taken off all her clothes, which only meant her bikini bottom and short T-shirt , before she went in. I had only my conservative one-piece tank suit, which I now rolled off wetly into a lump, and a towel which I wrapped tightly around me until I was warmer.

After a few minutes however, having gotten my breath back, I thought that I would try the shallower pool. I edged down to it and put in a foot. There was only about four inches of water, and it was warm. I sat at the edge of the pool and put my feet in. I looked at the small animal life that was flourishing there; found a crab and several snails. I had not put my wet suit back on, and now the sun beat down on my back. In a minute I would have to smear on sunscreen, for I was fair and burned easily, but for just this minute the warmth was seductive. Behind me I could hear the strength and movement of the sea, slapping lightly and then harder at the rocks, a rhythm that went on unceasingly and yet always with new variations, softer, softer, now harder, harder, harder.

"Anne," called Monika.

She was standing on a rock directly above me, still wet from her swim, the water dripping off her brown-and-gold triangle and down her legs. Her hair was streaked back from her forehead and she was drying her ears with the towel.

"Anne," she said again, more forcefully, and pointed behind me.

But I didn't turn for an instant, didn't understand. I simply sat and stared up at her, at her dripping body, brown all over, at her triangle almost above me, at her finger pointing.

Only at the last second did I turn and face the sudden large wave, which roared up the side of the rocks and hit me full in the face with a cold sweet hand. I had my mouth open somehow, perhaps in surprise, and so I swallowed some of it, and it got in my eyes and my nose. And yet, this time, it was not such a shock. In a strange way, it was exhilarating, this smack, this drenching, this sudden flare of cold in a hot world. It was like waking up, like being kicked into being more alive.

"Oh," I said, when I could speak, and then "Oh" several times as I could see another large wave forming. I jumped up and scrambled to where Monika stood, laughing at me, and watched the next wave hit where I had been.

It must have been the second day that I began to draw. I had not really had a plan for this visit. I'd brought my notes on Harriet and Kitty, and perhaps thought I could do some work on my monograph. But the parlor downstairs was dark during the day and musty. Out of curiosity I explored the shelves and flipped through the journals. They had yellowed paper covers, old-fashioned type, a formal feel. A few had penciled comments in the margins. I looked at the sepia and the black-and-white photographs on the walls, many of which dated from the early part of the century. The island had had fewer houses then, the harbor sailing ships. Trunks and kegs and wooden boxes of salt cod were piled at the dockside. In those days the house had seemed to burst at the seams with family and friends, prosperous, sturdy blond Swedes on summer holiday, in beautiful Edwardian dress that gave over to French-style striped shirts, baggy white cotton trousers, and espadrilles.

I read a little, stared out at the windows, tried to understand where I was and what world I had walked into. Then I took a walk around the island, which took less than an hour, it was so small. I sat in the tiny café and wrote a postcard to my parents and one to Astrid, and one more to my cousin Nancy. Then I went back to the house and asked Monika to give me a sketchbook.

I was shy about using even a pencil at first. I had hardly drawn for years. Once, as a child, my hands had told me what I saw in the world, but later everything went through my eyes and was given a name and a date and a history. I learned to talk about brush strokes without feeling a brush in my fingers, about contour and mass without touching or trying to describe that touch except though my vision. I learned, for research purposes and in order to teach students who had never held a brush, to focus on paintings for their subject matter more than their style.

Students were always interested in biographies, and I had come to think biographically too, especially as I began to resurrect the lives of the forgotten women who'd painted the pictures I was studying.

So my earliest sketches in Monika's studio, done sitting in a corner of the room on a stool, were feeble and unsure. My first drawing of her was little better than a nursery-school stick figure. My first attempt to recall the rules of perspective made the windows behind her look like flying carpets. My first reaching back into what I had known of how to create volume and mass through the use of shadowing—not what I knew intellectually—resulted in shells that looked like alien spacecraft. I hid those first drawings and kept working, remembering back through my fingers to how I'd drawn, as a child and an adolescent, before I learned too much about what art should be.

Monika paid no attention to me. She was utterly absorbed and lost to everything but the canvas before her. All year she taught art in a primary school. Summer was her time to do her own painting. She set up her easel before the window that faced the sea, but she didn't paint the sea. Neither of us painted the sea. Monika painted from objects on a table covered with stiff white butcher's paper, mostly seashells, and from drawings and photos of seashells.

That first summer I was there, she was still working on a series of paintings of islands and shells. Sometimes the shell was large and the island hidden inside it, sometimes the shells lay in a broken mass of fragments at the bottom of the picture while the island loomed very large above, and sometimes the shells seemed to be whirling above the island in an aerial and threatening perspective, but usually the color harmonies were the same—thin blue background, shells (usually some sort of conch or cowrie) painted very meticulously in pinks, whites, and pale yellows with accents of brown-orange, and the island always gray and rocky and lifeless, closed in upon itself like a fist. Perhaps lifeless is the wrong word. The island rocks had a magical quality of stillness.

I sketched and painted Monika. At her easel, at the table, with the windows behind her, with her seashells. Sometimes I used charcoal or pastel; one day I did a watercolor series; often I simply scribbled in pencil and ink. This was how I got to know her body, for after the first halfhearted attempt to cover herself politely, she went back to wearing what she usually wore in summer to paint, which was precisely nothing.

That's how I saw her, how she allowed me to see her. Nothing hidden, nothing pretend. Narrow, slightly rounded shoulders, a faint hump beginning below the back of her neck. Not much hair, just the simple triangle and two soft patches under her arms. Long fingers and toes, with a high arch in her foot. High apple-like breasts with brown nipples, a rounded belly like a little girl's, with an outie belly button. A long scar on one forearm, a compound fracture after falling from a tree when she was eight, and another scar, a little white one on her forehead from a piece of flying glass, a car accident in her teens.

Her brown hair was streaked with gold, and she usually wore it in a simple ponytail when working, sometimes with a band around her forehead to keep the wisps out of her eyes. I've described before her green eyes and oval face. Her nose was bent a little to one side, the nostrils flared easily; it was a small oddity, it made her look feral, as if she were sniffing the air. She had asthma and said that as a child it had been quite bad, but that now she was mainly fine, though sometimes she could have trouble catching her breath and she was still plagued by hay fever and sinus problems. That's why the ocean air was so good for her in summer. Perhaps because of her asthma, her lips were often slightly parted, the better to breathe. Those parted lips, never dry, always moist even without lipstick, were what I had the most trouble with. I would look and look at them, never able to get the shape quite right; I would usually make them too sweet, too bow-shaped.

I often though of Dürer when I drew her, or Lucas Cranach. Those luminous, translucent eyes, that neck that looked like it might snap in the breeze, those breasts that sat so high on the rib cage. That protective modesty of expression, that oval face, those narrow shoulders, all were of the German Renaissance and went oddly with her complete lack of interest in wearing clothes.

She was a good subject for me in that she never moved too quickly or abruptly, but always with economy and simplicity. She was a slow and careful painter. Two or three brush strokes and then she put the brush down, stepped back and considered. That same ease and focus was also how she went through her day. She habitually woke up early, around 6, and had a cup of black tea with milk. She did something in the garden for half an hour that looked like tai chi, but that she told me was bioenergetics. It was a way, she said without explaining, of dealing with past losses and unlocking tension and opening channels. A quiet but forceful sound came out of her when she did these exercises, something like "Ha-a-ach!" Afterward, with another cup of tea and a slice of bread and cheese, she went up to her studio. She was always at work by 7, and sometimes even earlier. I joined her later, but as the days went on, I rose earlier too and with more excitement. I could hardly wait to get to the studio myself. On waking I would always put my head out my window and take deep lungfuls of the sea air, and the salt wind would burn a little as I took it in.

We rarely spoke while we were working, but when it came time for lunch, at noon or 1, she had me look at her work for the morning and would ask me what I thought. Occasionally I showed her my sketches. One day I remarked how familiar it seemed, visually, to draw her standing before the open window.

"So many 19th-century paintings show a woman in front of a window. In the foreground it's terribly cozy and bourgeois: green plants, pictures on the walls, chairs and tables with tea sets. What could they want that wasn't inside that room? They have their book, their piano, their sewing. And yet the figures always look pensive and confined. Outside is the world, glowing with light, strangely distant and blurred. The window is open, yet they can't get to what is out there. Being women, they were trapped and passive."

"Don't you think it's still true?" asked Monika, not turning her eyes from her painting. "Here we are, two women, inside, while the beautiful world is out there."

"It can't have the same meaning now, now that we're free to choose whether to stand in front of the window or to go out."

"Are we so free?" she said.

"Well, of course," I answered, and began to go into all the

obvious ways in which the feminist movement of the last decade or more had given us new possibilities.

Monika listened politely—or perhaps she didn't listen at all. For after I had finished my long exposition, she merely said, "I think we still look out the window and want what we cannot have."

In the afternoons we sunbathed by the rocks and pools or took trips to the other islands with battered bikes she pulled out from her small basement. Monika, who paid so much attention to the details of life, would make us sandwiches, smoked salmon and cucumbers, Jarlsberg and sharp mustard, for these outings and would take along bottles of water into which she'd lightly squeezed lemon. If we passed a café, we had an ice cream and a coffee with cream, sitting outside.

One afternoon, two days before I was to leave, we took a long bike trip. Usually Monika could go faster and longer than I could. But that day, perhaps because it was very hot or perhaps because we went too far, she became very tired. She began to cough and to gasp, to have trouble breathing. I could hardly get her on the ferry and had to leave the two bikes at the harbor, leaning against a post, while I supported her home.

"What can I do?" I kept asking. "Shall I call a doctor?"

"No, no," she kept saying, between gasps. "There's no doctor here." And then when she could speak a little easier she explained, "It's just my asthma. I usually don't have it here. I don't understand. It was just a little too much today."

At the house she took some medication and used an inhaler, and lay down. When she got up for dinner, she was fine. After

I had helped her to her bed, I went back down to retrieve the bikes and bought some smoked shrimp and new potatoes at the market. I was worried about Monika, but still I had a kind of singing feeling in my veins. I had supported her up the hill, had held her brown sweaty body close to mine. I could still feel her skin on my palms.

That evening we had dinner in the garden. I did everything the way Monika would have: put a checked tablecloth on the table, set out mismatched good china, fit new candles into the tarnished silver holders. I went down to her cellar and pulled out a bottle of cool white German wine. Every year, she said, she brought a case of it from home. I boiled the potatoes and sprinkled them with dill from the garden and arranged the shrimp on butter lettuce leaves. I cut thin slices of rye bread and put out cheese and butter.

"How lovely," she said, when she came down, breathing normally, her nostrils only a little flared. She had on the cream knit shirt I remembered from the Oslo gallery, and her brown-gold hair was pulled back in a knot. "How lovely of you to make this for me. It's good, isn't it, to make things beautiful, all the details of life, to make them right."

I was thinking, *See, I can be the way you want. I can be like you.*

The evening was warm, and in the garden we were protected from the wind. We stayed there late, lighting the candles at 11, though they were still hardly necessary, drinking one bottle and then another. Monika talked about living alone in Germany, how it was different there than here. "In Cologne I often find myself lonely, but here I rarely am. There the phone rings and there are letters and I go out with friends, but I'm lonely all the same. Here nothing ever happens, sometimes I go days without talking to a soul, and yet I never feel odd about it."

"I can imagine that you have a lot of friends," I said. I was really very curious about her life in Cologne.

"Not many. It's so much work, keeping up with people, and then they feel bad that you don't call them. Sometimes I'd prefer to spend the evening by myself, even though I know I will not get any work done, and that in a way I will feel miserable knowing my friends are out having fun without me. But being alone is the only way I know to keep the channel open to my imagination. Painting, even not painting but thinking about painting involves a great deal of solitude."

"Tell me about your flat in Cologne."

"It's not like this," she said. "This is a magic place. There, well, it's neither old nor modern, the building comes from the '50s and has a kind of square solidity to it. I have a room for my painting, not a proper atelier, because of the light, but still filled with my paintings and art supplies. I have a chair there, and often in the evening I just go there and close the door to the rest of the apartment. I will sit reading something, poetry perhaps, or letters between writers or artists. There is a window overlooking the garden. And I will dream of being here, in summer, and of the sea."

"It sounds very romantic to me," I said.

"*You* are the romantic one, not I," said Monika, smiling. "For me, being alone is partly a matter of habit and partly one of practicality. Perhaps it's also been a kind of burden that I wish to throw off—this reluctance, this loneliness."

"Then how am I romantic?" I said. "I often feel the same things."

"You're romantic because you think that feminism can somehow solve this feeling of loneliness that we all as human beings share. You dream of a kind of utopia where women could be both alone and together."

"Why is that a utopia? Woman have managed it in the past. I'm sure there are many women still trying it today."

"If you believe in this utopia, then why aren't you trying to live it?"

"Well, because, you know that I, because of where I live and teach..." I stumbled. I certainly couldn't say to Monika that I thought she and I had been living it this past week.

"No, you are not *not* living it because you live in some tiny town in Minnesota. You are not living it because it is an impossible dream. You imagine that Harriet Backer and Kitty Kielland and their group had something of what you want—but you only imagine it because you don't know anything about what their real lives were like."

"No, that's not true. I do know quite a bit about their lives, and there's no reason to suppose they didn't successfully blend close companionship and a strong network of colleagues with plenty of time alone. Their work itself has a very solitary look to it. The landscapes Kitty did look as if there's no one else around for miles, and Harriet is constantly showing a woman seated by herself in a room somewhere, working, reading, playing the piano."

Monika pulled apart her bread. "It's good when you defend yourself," she said. "It's good you want to fight me a little."

"I don't want to fight you!' I said. "I want..."

"What? What do you want from me."

To be the Harriet to your Kitty? I couldn't tell her that. "I don't want anything."

"That's good," she said. "That's for the best. Don't ask anything from me. Then you won't be disappointed." She smiled as if she were joking, but her eyes were serious.

While we had been sitting there, past 11, a stiff little wind had come up. We went into the parlor, and Monika lit a coal fire. She began to tell me about the photographs on the walls.

"This is all my mother's family. A typical bourgeois Swedish family. They were in shipping in Göteborg and built this house to spend summers in. In earlier times there were lots of kids, but my grandparents only had two, my uncle Edvard and my mother. The house isn't really mine, you know. It still belongs to Edvard. He's rather old now, about 75, so he doesn't come out here much. He lives in Stockholm."

"You said he lived here once?"

"Yes, for a time in the '50s. He was getting a divorce and was having some kind of breakdown, I suppose. He announced to his family that he was finally going to write his great novel. But he did no novel writing that anyone has ever seen. Instead he wrote a book here about Swedish literature. It's a very cruel book," she added. "He was reviled across the country, and that made him feel better. He made a full recovery. His daughter Sara is the member of the family I'm closest to; the rest of the family—" Monika broke off and straightened one picture and then another. Then she went on, "They treated my mother very badly after the war. Of course everybody hated the Germans, and then my mother went and married one!"

"Was your father in the war?"

"No, his family put him in school in Sweden so he would be safe, and then he went on to study at Göteborg. That's where he and my mother met. He was not a soldier. He was not a Nazi. He was not in Germany during the war. But my father was German, and that was enough for my mother's family."

"And you're the only daughter. Do you feel Swedish or German?"

"If I had a choice I'd be neither," Monika said. "I'd be something nice, like a Laplander or Cherokee Indian. But I'm afraid I have no choice. Your family, what is it?"

"Scottish and Norwegian," I said, offhand. My family was completely uninteresting, compared to hers.

"If I had a choice," said Monika, "I would live in a place that had no nationality, that was not even on the map."

"I looked on the map when I planned to come here," I said. "And I didn't find this island."

Monika looked pleased. "You see? Perhaps it's happening already."

That night she told me about something that had happened to her as a child. She had been only two years old. The war had been over for a few years, but the economy was still shaky. Her parents were in their 20s, unsure about their parenting. Monika had gotten tuberculosis. She went to the hospital and was transferred to a special TB hospital for children in another city. She was to stay there for 18 months.

Her parents never came to visit her.

Afterward her mother would say that they had been told not to visit. Afterward her father would explain how poor they were. To take the train to this city far away, to have to find lodging and meals, to take off time from work (he was just rising in his field as a petrochemical engineer), all this was difficult if not impossible.

"It wasn't until years later that I realized my mother had come from a wealthy Swedish family. They would have certainly made it possible for her to visit me or to stay in the city where I was. But the family quarrel had not been made up then, and she didn't want to ask them for help.

"They say that I cried very much when they left me at the hospital, but that after that I didn't cry at all. The nurses wrote to them and said what a good child I was. I took my medicine and obeyed all the rules. And I never cried at all.

"When I was cured and they came to collect me at the hospital, I was almost four. I didn't know who they were. I didn't want to go with them. The hospital and the nurses were all I remembered, all I knew. 'Imagine that,' my mother will say. 'Monika didn't even know her own parents.' "

Painting is lovemaking, Picasso said somewhere, and as a feminist art historian I despised him for saying it. When I taught even my most basic Introduction to Art History courses, I tried to alert my students to the fact that the heroic male artists made use of women's bodies in particular ways, which led to a dichotomy of men as artists, women as subjects. "Ripe fruit," Renoir called his models. Other artists called them worse.

But with the charcoal or the brush in my hands, my fingers moving about the page, I understood, in a way I never had before, that drawing is a kind of touching, a kind of sexual touching that, while not the same as lovemaking, is certainly near to it. To make a flowing mark on the page is not so different from running a finger along the slope of a shoulder, over the roundness of a breast, down to the softness of a belly, the curve of a hip.

I don't know now, looking back, if Monika was indifferent to my constant scrutiny or whether she only pretended that she was. At the end of the day she would sometimes look at my drawings of her, but all she would say was "Good" or "You're improving."

She never drew me of course, and I kept my clothes on when I worked. For me to remove them would have had a different meaning. A sexual meaning. It would have been a sign that I wanted her.

Her nudity was not a sign. At least, not enough of one for me to be sure.

On the last evening of my visit we took a walk to the sea, down to the two pools. We had in fact spent a large part of the afternoon there, because it was so hot, and I had gotten more sunburned than I should have. I felt a little feverish, though that might have also been due to drinking more German wine at dinner. When we clambered over the rocks, they were still warm, and we lay down to watch the sky and sea. The sun, even at 10 o'clock, was very far from going down. I was warm through and through, and yet the slightest breeze kept tickling the surface of my skin.

We lay there and talked about all kinds of things in the most easy, friendly way possible, and still I kept a hold on myself, still I watched what I revealed.

"Do you ever think about having children?" she asked.

"Well…no." All week I had wanted to come out to her, but I couldn't find words that I didn't think might scare her off. These days past had been so perfect, so fragile and magic, that I didn't want to break their spell. I wanted to do nothing that was not natural for both of us.

"Like your women artists of the 19th century," she teased. "Career and children are incompatible."

"Without a...partner, it would be difficult," I said. "In 20th-century America."

"I find myself thinking of a child more than a partner. I suppose I would like to know what it feels like. Pregnancy. But I don't know if I would be a good mother."

"You must like children," I said, "to work with them every day."

"I don't know if I like children so much.," she said calmly. "I like the part of them I see when we make art together. But would I like to be a mother—all that noise and disruption? That's the question. I don't suppose I will ever find out."

A few moments passed. The sky was turning pink and yellow, like the luminous interior of one of her shells.

"Are you…" I had to ask, "seeing anyone?"

There was a silence, then she said calmly, "A man, you mean? Oh no. I think those days are over. They were always so serious, those German men. Swedes too. People say men don't want commitment; that's a lie. They are dying to get married and have you wash their socks."

I laughed, unreasonably happy. "Why don't we have one last swim?"

We took off our clothes and jumped, one after the other, in the larger, vase-shaped pool. As always the coldness took my breath away. "I thought it would have warmed up during the day."

"This one never warms up," she said. "Because it's deeper and because the channel goes directly into the sea. It's always filled with fresh water."

"Salt water."

"Yes, fresh salt water."

I wanted to get out immediately as I usually did, but forced myself to stay. And then a strange thing happened. The water began to feel not exactly warmer, but more familiar to me. My limbs were all outlined with cold, as if I were a pencil drawing, but inside the lines my body was lush and swollen. My arm brushed against Monika's, and my leg, and it was as if the pencil edges broke and smeared. How warm she was. She came around back of me and pressed her body up against mine a moment. Her breasts were shells, her triangle a tickle of seaweed against the backs of my thighs.

"It's been very good for me, having you here," Monika said. "I will miss you when you're gone. Can't you stay longer?"

My younger sister was getting married in a week's time and I was supposed to be her maid of honor. I had to, there was no way out. I felt embarrassed to say this, though, to Monika. I said instead, "I could come back."

"Oh, you'll get busy."

"No, I won't."

"When I feel easy around someone, I feel almost normal," she said, and now she held my shoulders and let her body float up to the surface behind me as if I were a pole and she a flag. "As if the loneliness is just part of life, and not the whole thing."

"My ideal is Harriet Backer and Kitty Kielland," I said. "Two women, two artists, living together for most of their lives, yet having separate spheres. To me, that's what love—feminism—is all about."

"Oh, you and your feminism," Monika laughed, and let me go and swam away. She didn't say anything about love.

We were quiet then, happy, I think, even though I was also in pain, hot and cold at the same time, my mouth brushed with salt instead of sweetness. We paddled around the little pool by the sea in a world that was turning peach and rose and lemon yellow.

"I won't get out till you do," I said, teeth chattering.

"I'm never getting out."

So then I had to.

II. Interior With Woman

When I was a child, one of my favorite books was *The Four-Story Mistake* by Elizabeth Enright. It was the story of four children who moved into an old house in the country with their father and housekeeper. One day, as they were playing in a large room on the third floor, one of them, the ten-year-old girl Randy (who wanted to be an artist) noticed the shape of a door behind old wallpaper. Through the door was a secret room with a mysterious portrait of a little girl named Clarinda. A secret room, boarded up, invisible to most people, with a tragic romantic history—this idea had great appeal to me from an early age.

I always wanted to discover a place like that in our family's summer home, and thought that if any place had room for a secret it was that ramshackle old wooden house with its add-on sleeping porches and bathrooms, its storerooms turned into bedrooms, its plumbing helter-skelter and its attic full of enticing books and old clothes, all smelling of mildew, and inhabited (less enticingly) by a colony of bats. I had worked out that the secret room must be up near the roof, in a space between some closets on the third floor and the back stair that led up to the attic. The walls by the staircase were some kind of knotty wood. How many hours I spent on those stairs meticulously pressing each knot, sure that if I pressed the right one, the panels would turn into a door I hadn't seen, a door that would open into the secret room.

I knew how the room would look; it would be small and uncluttered except for a single bed and dresser. It would be rather dark, but not frighteningly so. A narrow window that people would have always supposed was part of the attic would provide enough light to read by. I would fix up this room very stealthily, bringing sheets and pillows, and decorating it with my own crayon pictures and with some reproductions of old masters whose books I had found moldering in the attic. In this room I would be alone yet not alone. I would be surrounded by my family's noises and that would be comforting, but at the same time no one would know where I was, and no one would pay attention to me.

I thought back on this imaginary room, never discovered, when I was at the lake after my sister's wedding.

"You'll have your turn," one of my grandmothers was assuring me, in the same saccharine and possibly pessimistic tone in which my sister Betsy had said, while she was getting into her wedding gown this morning, "Oh, Annie, I wish it was you. I never thought I'd be first!"

Grandma Strand and I were sitting on the front porch, surrounded by relatives who had the same name, the same store of jokes, and the same warmly upbeat but slightly doubting way of looking at things. I didn't bother to answer her.

The only person I was completely out to was a younger cousin, Bobbie, now called Robert, who was gay and lived in New York and never came home. The rest of the family just thought I was a career woman. Because they remembered me dating boys in high school and because an old boyfriend used to accompany me to some family gatherings years ago, they assumed that I was straight, but too busy, or too picky, or perhaps, now that I was over 30, just too old to attract a man.

The wedding at the little local Lutheran church was over and the reception was well under way. My face was stiff from having smiled so much and agreed so many times that my sister was perfectly lovely and that she couldn't have found a better man. Dirk, his name was. I hardly knew him and didn't like him. But perhaps that wasn't fair, for I didn't like anybody much that day. I was hot and miserable in my perspiration-stained satin dress with its scratchy petticoat (petticoat, me!), stockings, and tight shoes. I kept trying to see the event through the eyes of Ingmar Bergman, as in *Fanny and Alexander,* when the eccentric extended family gathers for a large party. I was in fact trying to see my family through Monika Diechmann's eyes and to make them more interesting than they were.

She had an Uncle Edvard, a literary critic, a would-be novelist, a romantic depressive sitting on an island in the middle of winter, wearing a dressing gown and smoking a cigar while he wrote elegant hatchet jobs on all the writers of his time.

I had my Uncle Luke, Nancy's father, the insurance salesman, heavy and red-faced and eternally good-natured, and at the moment engaged in getting all the kids organized to play croquet in teams on the lawn that sloped down to the lake. Jackets had come off, and shoes; grass stains abounded. It was not Bergman, it was not a gathering of the children of Swedish bourgeoisie in sailor suits with short pants and frilly lawn and lace dresses. This was more like a swarm of puppies, the same sort of swarm I remembered once being part of.

The grandmother beside me, who was Luke's mother, said, "Oh, that boy was a ringleader from the moment he was born!"

I had never been a ringleader in my puppy swarm, where the definition of ringleader was probably "a born organizer." It was, however, generally acknowledged that I had some special gifts. I could draw better and swim faster than many of them and I was considered, though small for my age, rather peppy and "go get 'em." In that large, loving, extended family of mine, there was room for little quirks, small eccentricities, and modest talents. There was no room for major deviations like joining a cult, trading brilliantly on the stock exchange, becoming a serial killer, or living as a lesbian.

Now Nancy appeared on the porch and pulled up a chair, with the original comment, "Isn't it *hot*?" She pulled off her heels and waggled her toes. "*Much* better."

When Nancy and I were six or eight, or even 11, people often confused us. And that was not so much because we looked alike—Nancy was a brawny, freckled towhead and I was blond and slight—but because of aspirations to a similar noise level and energy and physical bravado of a kind then called tomboyish. I saw her regularly from an early age and every day during summer. Even now she was still the person I talked to, or tried to talk to, about some of the things that were important to me.

Like me she was 32. She had three children and ran a small day care business from her home. She often looked frazzled, but as if she enjoyed it. "I never have a minute to myself" she had been saying for the last five years, in a manner that was more proud than frustrated. "Half the time I can't remember who's president [this was at the beginning of the awful Reagan Revolution], and I never read the newspaper." She was indulgent, though occasionally impatient toward me, as I was toward her. One of the main things I had come to appreciate about her is that she never asked me if I was seeing anyone or when I was going to get married. I assumed she knew.

In the past she had supported me in all my strange desires—to get a Ph.D., to specialize in Scandinavian artists, and then to focus exclusively on Norwegian women painters—and today I had been longing to tell her about my trip to Norway and Sweden and my meeting with Monika, but Nan was more intent on describing her recent miscarriage.

"I suppose it's for the best," she said. "I already have the other kids and we really can't afford any more, but it was still a shock. At three months they already look like…little babies. I knew that but I hadn't *known* that. It certainly makes me more sympathetic to the pro-life movement...."

Still big and freckled, Nan wiggled out of her panty hose and told us all the bloody details, and they were bloody. Grandma Strand kept saying, "Oh, my, it's just like the miscarriage your mother had before you were born," and then just as Nan finished, another cousin came up and the whole story began again.

"I think I'll take a swim, I'm boiling," I told my grandmother.

"But you look so pretty in your blue dress. It's not often we get to see you looking so…pretty. And there's going to be dancing later, I've heard. And Dirk has some friends here that I'm sure would be delighted…"

I got up mid sentence and left them on the porch. Ten minutes later I was in the lake, precipitating a general exodus from the croquet game, as all the kids decided to join me. I played with them a little and then swam across the lake (it wasn't very big) to a stand of trees I remembered and hauled myself onto the bank. I was muddy all over and hot again within a few moments, with mosquitoes swarming around me. Oh, if just for an instant I could be back in that bracing salt water off the coast of Sweden, if I could lie on a hard warm rock drying in the wind, if I could stand, once more, in Monika's studio seeing her at the window with the thin curtains behind her.

The lake, which I had loved so much as a child and never more than when it was swarming with other kids, was like a tepid bathtub, dark green and murky.

At the risk of being called sulky and antisocial, I left the wedding party and the lake early the next morning, pleading some imaginary deadline. I had done a lot of research in Norway, I explained to my parents, and now I needed to write it all up. My father protested, "Annie, it's unhealthy to work as much as you do." My mother just sighed. She thought that I was behaving badly, but she looked as if she understood: sibling jealousy, as usual.

I had written Monika a light and friendly thank-you note the minute I stepped off the plane in Minneapolis, saying how sorry I was that I had to return to the States so soon and hinting that I would love to come back. As I drove home to the small town where I lived and taught, I couldn't help fantasizing that there would be a letter from Monika waiting for me. "Come back immediately," it would say. "I can't live without you."

Like all fantasies it was undeveloped in many ways. Would we live in Sweden or in Germany? How would I support myself? Would I teach—in German, in Germany? I didn't think through any of that. I only kept seeing myself, with the force of obsession, drawing Monika at the window of the studio, with the blue sea behind her. I only kept seeing her brown body, naked, next to me on a hot slab of stone, I only kept smelling her and hearing her and, though this was completely in imagination, tasting her salt skin and stroking her breasts.

There was no letter awaiting me at home, though one came in July. It was a bit formal, written on blue airmail paper with a fountain pen, in rounded letters. She spoke of her work, of having sold two paintings from the show in Oslo, of going to Göteborg twice for art supplies and then of being glad to get back to the island, where she could be alone, because that was what she loved about the island, her aloneness. But at the end, when I least expected it, after the coolness of most of the letter, the great emphasis on aloneness, Monika wrote: "It surprises me when I think that I invited you, a total stranger, into my house here, and that we got along so well. I have never invited anyone before. And I *never* had anyone work with me in my atelier. Maybe I am changing!"

I wrote back carefully, thanking her for everything. For the house, for the island, for giving me a sketchbook and encouragement to draw. I even thanked her for the weather. And I wrote about my own aloneness, and not wanting to be near my family, and about my research, and again about the island and how important it had been to me.

I reread this letter many times, then copied it over on to light green stationery (leaving out my gratitude over the weather), chose some interesting stamps, dropped it in the box.

For much of that long hot summer I neither unpacked my suitcases nor put away anything I'd bought in Norway or in Sweden: not the books or magazines, not the copied articles and letters, not the postcards and reproductions. I simply left them around the apartment or piled them on my desk haphazardly. In the midst of the confusion on the desk I made a kind of shrine of a rock from Monika's island, a shell that I had stolen off a table in her studio, and a photograph of the two pools by the ocean, with Monika lying on her back alongside the larger one. On the bulletin board above the desk I stuck postcards and reproductions of Harriet's and Kitty's paintings as well as one of Oda Krohg's. I pinned them over old announcements from my department, phone messages, and news clippings from my mother.

I don't know why, but at the time this chaotic arrangement appealed to me, even seemed necessary. I was always losing things and finding them again, very inefficiently. When I wanted to work at the desk, I simply pushed aside everything else and started. Occasionally my hand would brush against the shell or a ferry schedule from the Swedish archipelago, or I would find a receipt from a bookstore in Bergen or an Oslo tram ticket inside a book. All these things made me feel that I wasn't quite at home yet. That I didn't have to come back here. That I wasn't back.

I sat at my desk and worked. The monograph was not finished, but I was trying to write a paper to deliver in the fall and some shorter pieces. One of my colleagues had a sister called Evie Parkins, who was the editor of a feminist cultural journal in Minneapolis. One day I got a letter from Evie, asking me to write something about Harriet Backer and Kitty Kielland, as *Demeter* was doing a special issue on women and the visual arts. Evie wrote:

"My sister tells me that you've done a lot of research on these two women artists who managed to support themselves from their work and to live together. They sound fascinating!

The question we are interested in exploring in this issue of *Demeter* is: What are the conditions that make possible the artistic life of women? We're trying to focus on women artists who weren't related to, married to, or protégés of famous men (there aren't many), so Harriet Backer and Kitty Kielland sound perfect. If you could write about them and also (briefly) discuss the differences between 19th-century women and 20th-women artists from an economic and political viewpoint, that would be great!"

I sat at my desk and wrote at the top of the page:

What are the conditions that make possible the artistic life of women?

And then I wrote down:

Money

Time

Freedom

After a short pause I added "Emotional Support." It wasn't quite the word or the idea I wanted, but I didn't know what else to call it.

Then I began with a sort of general background, to the effect that in the 19th century only the European and North American bourgeoisie could afford to give their unmarried daughters art lessons and to support them while they studied in Paris or Munich. Eventually some of the women did become self-supporting, as portraitists usually, but for most of them art was a class luxury. Working-class women had no access to private courses or art academies, of course. What was unusual about the situation in Norway is that this country, which had only come into being in 1814 (it had previously been annexed to Denmark), had no tradition of excluding women, because it had so few traditions. This perhaps accounted for the strong network of women artists that grew up in the second half of the 19th century.

Harriet Backer was born in 1845. She grew up in a family of four sisters, all of whom were considered artistic, especially the second sister, Agathe, who played the piano. When Harriet was 25, after having had various art instructors in Christiania (now Oslo), she and Agathe traveled through Italy and Germany. During this time Harriet wrote several novels, none of which were published. Returning to Norway, she began to study at Knud Bergslien's school, and around the age of 30 made the decision to no longer be a dilettante, but to become a professional artist. To this end she set off with another woman to Munich and studied for four years. There she met Kitty Kielland and the two of them began to live together, as they would most of the rest of their lives. They spent ten years in Paris and then returned to Norway in 1889, where Harriet started an influential art school.

Harriet began with portraits, but gradually became more interested in the figure. Most of her paintings are of women seen indoors, often against a background of windows. Her early paintings from Germany are somber and often dark in the late romantic style, but after moving to Paris in 1878 she was influenced by the plein-air school and her palette lightened. Many of her best works have an iridescent quality of rooms suffused by light. She often chose craftswomen at work, weaving or sewing, or women reading by lamplight. These paintings have an appealing simplicity and earnestness, and are nationalistic in that they celebrate the specific quality of Norwegian life. They also have an interiority that can verge on the claustrophobic.

Kitty Kielland (1843–1914) received her first drawing lessons as a young girl, when she was ill and confined to a wheelchair for a period. Like Harriet she studied in Norway before traveling to Munich in search of further instruction and then on to Paris. Although Kitty painted their flat on the Left Bank, which was filled with flowers and paintings and plants, Kitty preferred landscapes to interiors, and even during her years abroad always went back to Norway during the summer to paint the countryside around Stavanger, especially the bogs, marshes, and windblown sand dunes. Kitty's landscapes are romantic, solitary, bleak, and as the years pass less realistic and more painterly. The light is often the light of the long summer nights in Norway. "Summer evening pictures," she called her work. *Sommernattsbilder.*

Kitty was the sister of the romantic poet Alexander Kielland, and sometimes in reviews of exhibits in which she participated she was called "Kielland's sister." She was not conventionally attractive, but rather had a "mannish expression." She was more openly feminist than Harriet and more apt to point out insults and omissions. In 1886 she wrote a sharp response to a pastor who had criticized unmarried women who tried to paint. It was published as *The Woman Question* and was bitterly attacked (one of the great criticisms against it was that Kitty was mannish and unattractive).

Harriet was a feminist too, but not as great an activist as Kitty. She said, "By concentrating [on my work] as a man does, I serve the woman's movement best." Nevertheless she was a strong role model for younger women, not only through the example of her work, but through creating a school where women artists could study freely. She was called "more than a woman painter" and "Norway's only woman painter" by male critics. She disliked both descriptions.

Were Harriet and Kitty lovers or romantic friends (here I introduced ideas from Carol Smith-Rosenberg's influential essay, "The Female World of Love and Ritual" and from Lillian Faderman's recently published book on female friendships and lesbian love, *Surpassing the Love of Men*), or just colleagues and roommates? There was really no way of knowing, and perhaps it didn't matter if we knew. They spent most of their adult lives together, and belonged to a larger circle of women artists. The network they helped create was composed of women who never married or had children and who supported each other as friends and sister professionals, allowing them to forge strong identities as artists.

It was a model that we in the 20th century could do well to emulate. These days we women had, theoretically, money, time, and freedom. In reality we could only have money if we took other jobs besides making art (something I had realized early on in college). We had jobs that kept us so busy we had no time for art, even if we wanted to make it. Freedom, yes, we could vote now and own property; we could even run for Congress. But as artists we still had a hard time getting shows or getting reviews. Only since the late '60s had women come together as self-identified feminist artists to develop projects such as the Women's Building in Los Angeles and to create works that were avowedly feminist for a feminist audience. I ended my article with a call for continuing to work for the liberation of all women and the liberation of ourselves as artists.

Yet, I spite of this inspiring rhetoric, the main question, "What are the conditions that make possible the artistic life of women?" still, to my mind, remained unanswered. If I had written my true feelings down, they might have looked more like this:

Love

Beauty

Joy

How could I put into words, much less economic and political terms, the memory of those perfect days on Monika's island, when each moment was infused with both peace and excitement? I had been awake and alive then, and I had held a pencil and a brush in my hand and made marks on paper, and outside the waves had dashed against the rock, and Monika had been there painting her seashells steadily. Emotional support? Money? Time? Freedom? What about the taste of salt water and the cool tang of white wine and the scent of climbing roses and the feel of the sun on my back? All those conditions had made art possible for us, two women, two women artists.

Evie called me promptly after I sent my article and said she liked it very much, especially for its discussion of romantic friendship ("Wouldn't it be great if we had more proof of women's relationships? I for one don't believe they were never sexual.") and for its upbeat ending. She would print it as is and would someday like to meet me. She sounded very young somehow, and I said only, "Sure, one of these days."

I wrote a letter to Monika and sent her my article. It was a lot to send, something I realized when I mailed the letter and the jovial postmistress said, "Do you want to send this book rate?" I received a letter back, finally, in August, saying it was her last week on the island and she had a great deal to do to get it ready for winter. She was packing up all her work and trying to figure out how to transport it down to the passenger ferry and by bus to Göteborg where she would then be able to ship it by train. "It's not like in the days of your Harriet and Kitty, when they had nice big steamer trunks and hired hands to carry them!" That was her only reference to H & K, but she did say, toward the end, that she was happy to hear I was making art again.

This took me aback a little. I hadn't made art all summer, had only written about it as usual. I had thanked her in my letter for giving me a sketchbook and encouragement, but in fact I had started and stopped in the course of my brief visit to the island. I hastily called around in Minneapolis until I found an evening course in life drawing that started in September. Then I wrote to Monika that I was seriously starting to draw the figure. I also wrote that I was planning a trip to Chicago to see an upcoming exhibit of Postimpressionists.

I was surprised at how nervous it made me even to shop for the things I needed for the drawing class: the charcoal sticks, the conte crayons, the newsprint pad. I hadn't taken an actual art class since college, and I was nervous about failing somehow. It had been different around Monika. I had been under her spell, and I had both pretended that I was an artist like her and also, knowing I was not, had let myself play. But a classroom situation was not play. It was serious. Everyone would be able to draw better than I could.

Of course it wasn't like that at all. Everyone was a beginner, just like me. Everyone had her own story of having dreamed of being an artist and of being afraid of failure. Everyone had his yearning to make something beautiful and real, her lovely human desire to make a picture of another human being. I was at ease from the first night, and each week got better. I drove up to the Twin Cities with my newsprint and charcoal and knew that when I drove home again, my fingers would be black and I would have a dozen or two dozen sketches, from ten-second poses to 20-minute ones. I learned to catch a gesture in the line of a shoulder or the bend of a knee. I learned to touch the outline of a breast as I sketched it on the page and feel the heft of a belly as I shadowed in its volume.

All that fall, on these drives to and from the Twin Cities, I thought about when I had stopped drawing, when I had become convinced that I had to make a decision about my future. The conventional answer would have been that I was someone who needed security, who needed a steady profession. The more interesting question was why I thought I had to answer "either/or" instead of "both."

I'd been the sort of child who drew pictures before she could read or write, whose drawings were always on the walls at school, if not at home. By junior high I'd given up my free and easy crayon pictures for tight, meticulously-drawn pen-and-ink architectural drawings and portraits of my friends. In high school, under Mrs. Hopkins's eye I experimented with clay sculpture and mixed media, as well as oils and pastels.

Even in my most secret being, however, I never said, "I want to be an artist," or more daringly, "I *am* an artist." I wanted someone—Mrs. Hopkins—to make the decision for me, to say, "Anne is one of the most talented girls I've ever come across. Send her right to New York!" Of course she didn't say that, however much she enjoyed working with me and praised my work. She was aware that I was academically gifted and was going on scholarship to Macalester College in St. Paul. She only said to me, "I hope you'll continue to take a few art courses, Anne."

I took her lack of encouragement in the same way I took the lack of feeling singled out in my college art classes (no girls were singled out, now that I think about it): as a sign that I wasn't really very good or original. I didn't have what it took. My art history professor, on the other hand, the charming, buxom Mrs. Traynor, was immediately impressed by my essays. Of such things are life choices made. All my life I'd drawn and painted and then, at 19, art became a mystery that had to be unraveled by words. I couldn't paint as Giotto or Cézanne had, but I could write about them.

Once every month or six weeks a letter arrived from Cologne, from Monika Diechmann. It would not be too much to say that I lived for those letters, those squarish blue envelopes with the handwritten thin pages inside, never less than two pages, sometimes as many as ten. Every day, opening the tiny door to my postbox in the lobby of the apartment building, I looked for blue. And if I saw it, my whole day would change. Would become radiant.

Usually Monika's letters began with the weather and some sense of where she was. Sometimes it was a café or a park bench, but usually it was her apartment. "I am sitting high up in my bedroom—five flights, one's leg muscles get very developed here—outside the snow falls. I have had a trying day at work, little children and all that. I know I should take up my paints or at least my pencil, but instead I sit here and drink my tea and watch the snow fall and think of you. Perhaps you are also watching the snow fall, and it must fall so much and so often in Minnesota. Perhaps you also are tired from a day of teaching and want your tea very badly...."

I had always been a coffee drinker, but now I took up tea even though I had to drive to the Twin Cities to find Assam, the kind Monika favored, and a silver-plated strainer and a round blue-and-white teapot and a white pitcher for milk, just like hers.

If there was a letter, I would make myself a pot of tea before I even opened it. I would take my precious blue envelope with its sober stamps over to the table and armchair by the window. Sometimes it was snowing; sometimes it was just biting cold or raining or bleak. But I would feel some magic from Monika emanating from the page. She very rarely mentioned friends or relatives; she never talked of anything she'd done socially; and she certainly didn't spend her postage money describing to me the political situation in Germany, fraught as it was (I sometimes read about it in the newspaper) with issues of immigration and asylum. No, Monika described the weather and her moods; she wrote about exhibits she'd seen or books she'd read. She quoted poetry, especially Rilke. She pondered her past, her persistent sense of her own aloneness, and tried to explain it to me.

In November she wrote:

> My knowledge that I was alone in the world came early. It came often at night in the hospital when I would wake up and hear the breathing of the other children in the ward and imagine that I was the only one awake.
>
> I passed long days in bed. It was not so much that I was too sick to play as that, according to the rules of the time, which must not be broken, I must have plenty of rest, and that meant in bed.
>
> It seems to me that I did not even know the meaning or purpose of my legs for a very long time. I was so used to seeing them only as two little sticks or two small mountain peaks under the covers, bedclothes that sometimes swirled around me like water, and sometimes were flat and straight as a desert. My hands were active, were allowed to be active, but moving my legs was the opposite of 'rest' and was forbidden.
>
> My parents had sent me a few toys, and the hospital had a few too. I could not amuse myself by reading, though I was sometimes read to, only by drawing, which I began early on, and by looking at things in a certain way. I had many stories about a certain crack in the wall. And quite a lot about a brown cloud in the ceiling, which I only realized years later must

> have been a water stain. I had so few things of my own to make stories with that anything that crossed my bed or that was visible from where I lay was very precious to me, a miracle. There were two things that I especially liked, a small car that I drove up and down the blankets, and a small conch shell that one of the nurses brought me.
>
> You will ask, What about the other children? Couldn't they have been my friends? Couldn't we have played together? But playing, that is, skipping, running, hopping—we couldn't do any of that. We could talk, but really, at three and four and younger, what could we say? Our beds felt very far away from each other. And then, there was a sort of rivalry for the attention of the nurses. I remember that I did not think it fair that the little girl whose mother came to visit her twice a week should also be allowed to have the nurse's affection.

She wrote at the end, "The loneliest thing to me is getting close to a person, because it makes me realize that you can never really get close, and you feel the separation, and it's painful."

"I know what you mean about loneliness," I wrote back immediately, reassuring her. "I think women artists have always had to be alone in order to create. But I think, finally, that is changing."

I wrote this out of my own loneliness, which was purely about missing her.

The fall passed. Thanksgiving came and went, and so did Christmas. I went to the home of one set of grandparents for the first holiday and to the other set's for the second. I avoided my sister and her new husband as much as possible. Even Nancy and I were on the outs. She didn't like the female nude drawing I gave her, framed in copper, as a Christmas present; I hated the sweater she had knit me. "Where am I going to hang this in the house?" she demanded. "With three children under ten?" I put the sweater in the back of my closet.

I had told only a few friends about Monika, mostly the straight women I'd pursued on and off for the five years I'd been teaching at the college. They were sweet about it and more than just a little skeptical. Not only about the obvious things—that I hardly knew this woman and that she lived in a foreign country—they grilled me most heavily on the question of why I assumed that Monika, who was probably straight, would be interested me other than as a friend. These women who kindly grilled me (Mary Lou the bouncy dance teacher, Debbie the French professor, Lois the historian specializing in the Renaissance) were the same women who had turned down my love or transformed my crushes into friendship. These were the same friends who urged me to go to the Twin Cities and find a lesbian bar or—since it was the beginning of the clean and sober movement—a coffeehouse. They advised answering an ad or running one, or joining a support group or starting one.

I ignored them.

Looking back, I see that my love for Monika was hopeless. I simply had no luck pursuing women. I was only successful when I stood still and let myself be caught. That's how I met my first lover, Jennifer, and Beth, my lover of six years now. It's probably also how I got together with Evie. Before Evie, before Beth, I thought that if I was patient and persistent enough in my loving, I could win over anyone. I could see that this goal failed with *individuals,* but since I felt always on the verge of success, I refused to see that there was any pattern to my failure.

I concentrated on externals. I pretended I was Jennifer, the professor at Champaign-Urbana who had brought me out as a graduate student. I cut my hair short. I wore plain white shirts and tweed jackets. I tried to exude an air of tough tenderness, of relentless, admiring persistence, and, when all else failed, vulnerability closely followed by whining. None of these strategies were remotely workable. My women colleagues simply shook their heads when the subject finally came up and said, "But you know I'm not gay, Anne," or "You know I have a boyfriend, Annie." Well, of course I knew that. But so what? I was prepared to wait them out, wait until they gave in or realized their essential nature.

Part of my problem of course was that straight women were my objects of desire. I did not choose them because they presented a great challenge, but because they were, of all gender-orientation groups, most familiar to me. After all, until I was 22 *I* had been heterosexual, more or less. I knew that I had made a switch and that, theoretically, any woman could do just the same, at any time. Moreover, because I had once been heterosexual, I knew how straight women thought. I knew the ways in which they thought about men, that there was loathing as well as attraction. I knew how they fantasized about women's bodies. I knew how they dreamed of transgression and passion.

I knew they had it in them.

"Why don't you just get yourself a lesbian girlfriend?" they said.

But that was probably far too obvious a solution.

"I draw a distinction between these three things," Monika wrote in January. "Solitude, loneliness, and isolation. I have felt them all, they are all part of my life, and they all are part of being alone, as I am. Solitude is of course the best. It is a condition for my work, and it is also a pleasure. It is about waking in the morning, early, and being able to go right to work. It is about not having to live my life to anyone else's pattern or demand, but being able to flow through the day according to my own rhythms. I especially feel it on the island, when I can think about my work all day long if I choose and dream about it at night.

"Loneliness is a much more frequent emotion. I can have it when I am alone, but I can also have it with other people. It never feels joyous, though it can sometimes have a melancholy to it that is somehow a nice feeling. I feel it in Cologne, say during my lunch hour when I am having my sandwich in the lunchroom and realize I have nothing to say to the people around me. Or I can feel it very strongly coming driving home and noticing people on the street, in couples. I might feel it when I'm trying to talk to a friend and she doesn't understand me. I have felt it after making love and especially in the morning. Loneliness is about feeling the gulf between me and others.

"Isolation is feeling that the gulf is an ocean. It is a very strange feeling, very physical, like there is something besides air between me and the world. It affects my face. It will make me unable to open my mouth, for instance, because I've forgotten how to speak. My limbs will feel heavy like lead. I will sit in my flat and the phone will ring and I will feel that not even through a great effort of will could I get up and answer it in human language. I look at that white phone, and I hear it ringing, but I can't form an image on the other end of someone I would like to talk to. It doesn't help me that there is someone calling me, someone who might care about me or ask me for dinner. I look at that phone with horror.

"This isolated feeling is very close to what I imagine insanity to be. I have had it all my life from time to time. Usually very short times, but occasionally it has lasted longer. The longest time was about a month. It was like Kierkegaard talked about, 'fear and loathing.' That was at art school. It was very bad. My cousin Sara came and got me and took me to the island. That's when I began staying there for the first time. That's when I found the differences between solitude, loneliness, and isolation."

This letter was in my box when I came home late one evening from my life drawing class in Minneapolis. The roads had been bad, for it was snowing hard, and I had been tensed up the whole drive back. When I found the blue envelope in the box, however, my spirit lightened—this, in spite of the fact that this letter was not particularly cheerful or personal. Actually it was personal, in the deepest way, if I chose to read it so. There were no concrete details in it, only the brief mention that she was writing it late at night, but I felt that I was seeing into Monika's soul, that she was allowing me to see into it. Later I thought, after everything was over and I read the letters again once more before putting them away, that letter could have been written to anyone. But at the time it seemed to speak directly to me.

It seemed to say, "I'm trusting you with my deepest feelings." It seemed to promise, "I want you to know all about me, even my worst fears." It seemed to say, "Dear Anne, are you like me? Can you love someone like me?"

I had gone upstairs and taken off my coat. I made myself a pot of tea and read the letter several times. I thought about how to answer her, and that made me think about whether I had known loneliness or isolation. I didn't think so, not really. I had lived with my parents till I was 18 and then in a dorm through college. In graduate school I had shared an apartment with two women in my department. These last five years were the first time I had lived alone. I had not liked it or disliked it particularly. I looked around and realized that I had not really seen this place for a couple of years. The first year I'd bought some used furniture, a couch and kitchen table and chairs—they still remained. My bedroom was usually a disaster zone. I rarely put away my clothes until it was time for the weekly (or monthly) wash, and I never made my bed. The kitchen was sort of the same, with dirty dishes always in the sink and the refrigerator full of moldy things in Tupperware.

I made a dispirited and then indignant tour of my little apartment. A so-called lover of art, and yet I hardly had a picture on the wall, only my jam-packed bulletin board and a calendar of women artists. This couch—disgustingly full of crumbs. I had never been messy as a child: it had come later, in college, when I had been so busy working and student teaching and studying. The life of the mind was all-important. And meanwhile I'd become a pig.

It may seem a strange response to Monika's letter about the varying states of aloneness that I would stay up half the night cleaning my apartment—and not just straightening up, but getting down on my hands and knees and scrubbing behind the toilet and the refrigerator—after all, I had never seen her flat in Cologne, but I knew that her island home was not the tidiest place, except for the bedrooms. Was I thinking, *What if Monika ever came to visit?* Did I suddenly realize I couldn't live like this anymore? Or was it about something else completely? Some way of taking my own life in my hands and looking at it, and not being satisfied with what I saw?

I stayed up half the night washing floors and vacuuming and going down to the basement to put clothes in the machines (the manager talked to me about all this the next morning). I remember that about 4 o'clock I happened to stop and look out the window. It had stopped snowing some time ago, and everything was very still and quiet. I could see the night sky, still with stars, and the white drifts of snow. My car was covered, and all those on the block. The lamp down the street gave off a very small glow, it seemed, and there were a few other lights over doorways and in windows. Otherwise it was dark, and very silent.

I thought about women standing in front of windows, being painted in front of windows, and then I decided to go out. I put a lot of clothes on, enough to stop the cold for just a minute. I went out into the snow drifts and looked up at the black sky with all its stars. What I felt that moment was a solitude like joy itself. Wide awake. The cold was like being slapped with a wave.

I wrote about that later to Monika. I did not tell her about the housecleaning exactly, but I did tell her that I had decided to turn my bedroom into a studio and to sleep on the folding bed in the living room.

Winter passed, slowly. Spring came, late. I continued to take the life drawing class and had gotten to know some of the other students. I also met Evie for the first time, when the issue of her journal came out and she invited me to have coffee and get my free copies.

"I want to marry aesthetics to politics," Evie told me earnestly that first meeting. We were in a bookstore café. Outside the slush of melting snow had made a river of the street. Our shoes were wet, and her hair was very curly under the cap she pulled off. I'd been right. She was younger than me, 25 as it turned out, with a younger person's energy and righteousness. "So many of our journals and newspapers are downright ugly," she went on, caressing the cover of *Demeter,* which featured a full-color reproduction of a Judy Chicago painting. "I want to change all that."

She was working as a typesetter and putting out the twice-yearly journal (it was some sort of collective but it sounded as if she did most of the work) evenings and weekends. She had big plans for this journal, she told me, which is why she'd taken this job as a typesetter—well, for money of course, because you had to eat, but it was mainly so that she could typeset the journal for free. The next issue was to be on work and money and the issue after that on lesbian writing and art. She hoped in conjunction with the lesbian issue to do readings and mount an exhibit in some local art gallery. Would I be interested in curating it?

"Maybe," I said vaguely, remembering that next year was when my tenure came up for review.

Evie was small and talkative. She always seemed to wear the same sweater, a dirty-rose one that her grandmother had knitted for her. She had the same sort of family I did—large, loving, and completely unremarkable. We got together from time to time through the late winter and spring. I went to a benefit reading for the journal and gave a brief talk at the university about Scandinavian women artists. Once or twice I helped Evie out with design questions for the upcoming issue. And eventually, although I had my doubts, I began to come to occasional meetings for the lesbian writing and art issue to help plan its design and content and to begin discussions for the art exhibit.

I had a full load of classes that spring semester, and I dropped my drawing class. *Demeter* was taking up some of my extra time, and I was also having some trouble with my chair that preoccupied me. He said he'd had some complaints that my teaching might be too "biased." That is, that I was talking about women artists too much.

"It may seem like I'm talking about women too much because I have to use sources that aren't in the usual texts," I explained. "Grombrich [the main textbook for my introductory classes] leaves out all sorts of important women painters, like Sofonssiba Aguissola and Artimeschia Gentileschi. And it's the same with my 19th-century course. The work of painters like Berthe Morisot, Mary Cassatt, Cecilia Beaux is hardly mentioned, much less all the Scandinavian painters. It's more work for me. I have to bring in other material and discuss some of the reasons why they aren't included in the standard books."

"You were hired to teach art history," he said. "Not feminist art history."

I wrote, complaining, to Monika about this rebuke and didn't get an answer, and told Evie about it too. She thought I should ignore him and start applying for other jobs. "Why do you want to teach in a place like that anyway?" she said. "You could teach anywhere."

She asked me over dinner. She lived in a small studio jammed with books and magazines, many of them unabashedly feminist and lesbian. She chattered all the time she cooked a splendid meal of vegetarian lasagna. She talked about the journal and about her own poetry (she read me some) and about her family and their reactions to her lesbianism. I found myself, though enjoying her company, not quite there. For today I'd received another letter, a short one from Monika, and my mind was still on it.

Anne,

I write to you still shaking after a very terrible encounter with my parents. I said things to them that I needed to say, but that do not make me happy.

It was their wedding anniversary, their 35th. The German relatives, my father's, were all there. None, as usual from Sweden. My mother's response was as it always is. Bravado. Scorn. Drinking a little too much wine. Pretending she would rather have this family, her husband's, than her own family—even though she secretly doesn't like them much.

And then my father being the patriarch of the house—pointing out all the new things since their last visit, in this case the very impressive new burglar alarm system, which will protect all these nice things they have.

I really couldn't bear it. The stuffiness, the self-congratulation, the hypocrisy about what a good marriage it is. The toasting and the food piled on the table, big slices of pork and cabbage.

And so, when it was time for me to make a toast, I got up and told them exactly what I thought.

I don't think I can ever go back there again.

But, perhaps, that is what I wanted.

Thank you for listening.

Monika

This thank-you was the nearest Monika had come so far to acknowledging that I had some role to play in her life, that I was important to her. And a part of my brain, even as I enjoyed Evie's lasagna and listened to her stories, was occupied in writing back to Monika.

To my surprise, Evie hugged me hard as I left her apartment. "You're such a great person to talk to, so understanding. I hope we can do this again sometime."

In my confusion, because I had stopped listening to her at least an hour before, I invited her to dinner at my place.

My apartment had changed in the last few months. I'd thrown out all but a couple pieces of furniture and bought a new table and chairs and a couch, in a Scandinavian style that was light and could be easily moved. I'd painted the kitchen yellow and now kept it very clean. On the living room walls I'd hung some framed posters of women's art and a few of my own figure drawings and paintings, including one watercolor of Monika. My desk was no longer a messy shrine, though I had found a place for the rock and the shell and the photograph on a shelf in my new studio, which had once been my bedroom.

"It's very artistic," Evie said, walking around. "It looks like you. Very disciplined and hard-working. And solitary. You seem like a person who needs a lot of space around her. Have you always lived alone?"

"No."

"So you think it's possible, two people sharing a life, each doing her own thing, supporting each other?"

"Of course," I said, not understanding her question or the slightly earnest emphasis of it.

But she stopped when she came to the shelf with the stone and shell and Monika's photograph. "Who's that?"

"A woman I met, an artist in Germany. That was taken last summer, on a Swedish island."

"What's her name?"

"Monika." I almost added, because I wanted to confide, that I thought I was in love with her, but refrained.

Still, after that, Evie would ask me from time to time about Monika, if we corresponded, if we planned to see each other again soon. And in spite of myself I would glow a little and said, "Yes" and "Yes, I hope so."

One day in April I got a postcard from Monika in the mail. A postcard was very unlike her, and so was the picture. It came from an island in Greece and showed a brilliant white house against a cobalt sea. "We have rented a house here for a month," she said. "I am doing a great deal of painting, as well as swimming and lying in the sun. How good it feels to have the sun on me again. I hope you are well."

I stood for a long time in front of my mailbox looking at this card. It seemed to be written in a language I didn't know and couldn't decipher. Monika had never written the word "we" before, not about anyone. Who was she with? A friend, a lover? A man, a woman? Even though I had read all her letters over 20 times at least, I got them out again and read them again, searching for some tiny sign that she had someone in her life besides me. There was none.

I was angry somehow. I wrote a letter to her address in Cologne expressing my discontent with not knowing her better. "It's frustrating," I wrote. "Not to have any idea who your friends are and how you live your life. We write so frequently and yet I sometimes feel I don't really know you." After I dropped this in the box I immediately felt awful, as if I'd ruined everything. I waited a few days and then wrote a perfectly normal letter, saying that my monograph was being published and that I had received an invitation to come to Norway the next fall and to participate in a seminar about Harriet Backer and her school.

I didn't hear from Monika for over two months, not until early July in fact. Her letter took no notice of my angry one, but she apologized for not writing sooner. "So much has happened," she wrote a little vaguely. "Big changes in my life. Getting ready to come to the island is always so much work (shipping by train all those canvases I shipped away last year, back on the bus, back on the ferry, up the hill—oh, you can imagine). But now I am safely here. The summer is a cool one so far. I remember last year (when you were here!) how hot and lovely it was. If you're in Norway this fall, why don't you come a little early and visit me in August?"

I was agitated until I read her final lines (with Monika the warmth always seemed to come in the final lines) and then I immediately called the travel agent. My presentation in Norway was not till October, but Monika didn't need to know that. I made my flight for the end of July, to Stockholm, so that I could be sure to arrive on Monika's doorstep August 1.

I took a box of art supplies with me and told everyone I was going to an island off the coast of Sweden for a month to stay with Monika, that artist friend of mine. Everyone was skeptical of this trip, except for Evie, who seemed sad while driving me to the airport. The only person I didn't inform of my trip was Monika.

"What is necessary, after all," Monika had written me once during the early spring, quoting to me from Rilke's *Letter to a*

Young Poet, "is only this: solitude, vast inner solitude. To walk inside yourself and meet no one for hours—that is what you must be able to attain."

But when I'd picked up the book, which I had not read before, I found another quote that suited me better. Love, wrote Rilke, consists in this: "that two solitudes protect and border and greet each other."

My solitude would greet Monika's solitude on her island; my love would surprise and enchant her.

III. Evening Landscapes

Sommernattsbilder. Aftenlandscaper. Pictures of summer nights and evening landscapes especially. That's what Kitty Kielland painted toward the end of her career. Those long light evenings that go on and go on, past midnight in the south of Norway and later still in north, until twilight turns into early morning. That it is light so late, that the sun is somewhere in the sky, doesn't always mean it's sunny. In Kitty's paintings there is no happy brightness. The light is often cold and diffused through clouds, and if a beam comes through it is a single beam that only underscores the light-leached quality of the trees and ground. The light fades and fades but never quite vanishes. The sun hovers and dips but never quite drops down decisively as it does nearer the equator. It is rather like the last guest at the party who stays on and on, past all winks and hints and yawns, still waiting for something to happen, still wanting something from the evening, now turning to morning, still hoping, when all hope is gone and everyone else departed, that the desire for connection will be fulfilled, the wish for love granted, the festive dream made real.

In Minnesota the beginning of August is still the very heart of summer. It had been sweltering and sticky as usual, and I had left it with relief, ready for the bright clean sun and salt wind of Monika's island. But Stockholm was gray and rainy, with already, unbelievably, something of autumn in the air, and I found more of the same in Göteborg. I boarded the ferry to A. mid afternoon under a lowering sky and barely saw the outline of the island as we approached. It looked forbidding and closed off, and although the harbor was full of pleasure craft, most people were wearing thick jackets and caps against the chill.

It wasn't that I hadn't tried calling Monika. I had tried from Stockholm yesterday and from Göteborg this morning. There had been no answer, however, and as I began the walk up to her house, my heavy rucksack on my back and my box of art supplies in my arms, I began to feel a sense of dread that I couldn't assuage with cheering thoughts: *She invited you, for God's sake. It is August. If she's not here, you can just...leave again. If she has someone here you can just...leave again. If she doesn't want you here...*but no, I couldn't let myself think that, not after all those letters.

The house, when I finally reached it, was little like my memory of it. In the cold light of a windy afternoon, with a storm approaching, the yellow was dull and washed out; the garden looked untended. And yet I could see a lamp on in the kitchen window and see the faint signs of habitation: a window slightly open, flies around the trash can, scuffed shoes by the door.

I set down my rucksack and my box, resisting the foolish urge to hide them behind a corner so it might look as if I were only dropping by, and gave a loud knock.

When Monika came to the door she was wearing a heavy sweater and slacks. Her hair was pulled back under a kerchief—the face seemed more egg-shaped than oval, the cheeks fuller. She looked different, though no less beautiful to me. Her eyes were still luminous and green, and although she was paler she was also rosier.

"Oh," she said. "It's you."

At least she seemed to recognize me.

My smile caught on my teeth. "I tried to call...you asked me to visit you when I was over here...if it's not convenient I can..."

"No, excuse my impoliteness. Please, come in. You're my guest, of course. I'm just....I thought it would be later. In August."

"It is August."

"Oh yes, of course. The time goes so quickly here. Come in."

In the confusion she did not give me a hug, so that our initial meeting, after all those months of longing, went by without a touch. I meant to hug her, but instead just handed her the box of expensive chocolates that I'd bought in Stockholm. They were Belgian with hazelnut and cream, shaped like tiny conchs and sea horses.

"Thank you," she said and put them on the table, where they later disappeared under a pile of newspapers, forgotten.

She was surprised to see me, but that didn't mean she wasn't also glad, I told myself as I followed her upstairs that day.

"Your same room, you see—just waiting for you. And I'll clear out a spot for you in the atelier. You've brought a whole box of art supplies, how lovely. Will you let me rummage? I love foreign materials. Come into the atelier when you're settled and let me show you what I've done this summer."

"My same room"—I thanked her for that. It was just as empty as I remembered, but a little more like a nun's cell without the sun dancing on its walls. I opened the shutters and looked out to sea. A greenish-black cloud sat on the horizon like a large toad. The wind had rain in it now, and it spattered my face coldly. It could have been November. I put my suitcase under the bed and sat on the edge of the bed a moment, trying to feel very glad I was finally here. I'd been traveling for two days, and now I was settled. Monika had been expecting me and was glad to see me. I had to believe that.

But all I felt was that I should not have come.

I put on another sweater and went to join Monika in the studio facing the sea. The windows were closed, and the long thin white curtains hung slack. There was a view of the same dark sky—the single green-black cloud had been joined by dozens more. But Monika of course paid no attention to the view. She had three canvases going, and her two work tables were cluttered with paints and brushes, and with many conchs and scallops in various sizes.

"What do you think?" she asked. She had arranged all her finished canvases in a row along the wall.

The canvases were larger than last year's, and Monika had filled the shallow pictorial plane with enormous translucent shell shapes, mostly scallop shells, fluted and cupped, and which held other, smaller scallops and conchs inside. Sometimes there were only one or two; sometimes there was a whole Chinese box series of shapes, one inside the next. They reminded me of Dale Chihuly's glass sculptures, which at that time I had seen only in photographs. That same sense of delicacy, of holding, of widening yet encompassing.

In this new series, for the most part, the island shape was absent; in two or three of the canvases it formed a pattern-motif around the edges of the canvases, just as the shells had once done. But the island was no longer the subject of the paintings. The shells were. As before, but even more strongly, the light source seemed to come from within the painting; everything radiated in a graduated, luminous light on the flat plane.

The island imagery diminished, the shells in the foreground, the shells containing one another—all these seemed positive signs. I went further and saw the conchs, pink and peach, as more flesh than shell, as Monika's tentative explorations of her own female sexuality. Although I did not say this to her, I saw the shape and color of the conchs as proof that Monika was moving toward the possibility of loving women. Of loving me. I did not mention this interpretation, however. I talked about her technique being much improved; I talked about the compositions as compositions. Only after we'd been talking for quite a long time did she ask if she could see my work, and I had to say I hadn't brought anything, it had not occurred to me to bring anything to show her, and anyway, most of it was on big blocks of newsprint. The fact was, since I'd stopped attending my life drawing class in May, I hadn't picked up a pen or piece of charcoal. Was it that I still needed outside stimulus, the camaraderie of a group of other beginners who admired my work? I tried to remember what I been doing since classes ended. Getting together with Evie for coffee, going to see my family at the lake, having to listen to my sister talk about her first pregnancy. Visiting Nancy and realizing we had nothing in common anymore and that I was sick of sitting there silent while she chattered about the new church she'd begun to attend. Mooning around all through July with the anticipation of being near Monika again.

"I hope to do some work while I'm here. To pick up where I left off," I said.

"What will you work on?"

"The figure is still what interests me most."

"That will be difficult for you here," she said, obviously forgetting that last summer I had drawn her and her alone. "No models," she explained. "Unless we could persuade one of those old fishermen to pose for you." She laughed and asked if she could look in my box of supplies. She was at ease, it seemed, where I was not. Last year I had looked at her with pleasure. Now my hands felt empty as I watched her bend over the box. I wanted to go up behind her and press my face into her heavy sweater.

"We will have a week like last year," she said. "Probably no swimming, but plenty of painting and maybe a bike ride or two."

I had not imagined I would only stay a week. "Like last year," I echoed forlornly.

"It's really been the most awful summer," she said over a dinner of fish and potatoes later. "That's why we have no lettuce or vegetables tonight. Nothing wants to grow in my garden. But on the other hand, it has been very good for my work. Oh, Anne, I have something to tell you!"

My heart stopped.

"Those big changes you spoke of in your letter?" I waited for the bad news. She was getting married. She had fallen in love with another woman.

"I've quit my teaching job! I took a leave of absence, went to Greece, and made my decision. There! Aren't you impressed? Somehow I just had to do it."

"But...how will you live?"

"Very simply. I won't live in Cologne any longer. Germany is far too expensive. I have given up my flat, my car, put some things in storage, and sold some other things. I'll live on the island four or five months of the year now instead of only three, from May through September. Won't that be fantastic?"

"Where will you live the rest of the year?"

"In Greece, on a Greek island! It can be cold there too in winter, but the light, Anne, the sun on the white buildings with the burning blue sky above, you have never seen anything like it. Later tonight, I'll show you the paintings I did there this spring."

In the candlelight her skin glowed and her eyes were the color of green sea foam. Her words were boring a hole through my heart, and that hole was expanding rapidly to become a huge empty cavern. Actually it wasn't empty at all: It was filled with the bitter comprehension that there was no place in this picture for me.

I didn't say anything; I even followed her upstairs and looked at her Greek pictures and tried to talk about them intelligently.

But as soon as I could, I excused myself, saying I was exhausted from my travel of the last two days. And then I lay for a long time in bed, listening to the storm come in.

It stormed for the next four days. As soon as one front passed, another surged toward us. Summer seemed to be over here; it was already early fall, chill and damp and dark. Monika had an electric heater in her studio, but in order for it to be effective, the door had to be kept closed. It was closed when I got up groggily the next morning, having slept in far too long, and when I finally got the courage to poke my nose in, I could see that she had not cleared off a space for me to work.

"Make yourself at home," she said, distracted, standing back from her canvas and continuing to look at it. "There's a fire in the parlor too. It may be warmer there, in fact."

I took my sketchbook from its box and went down to the parlor where the old tile stove was burning brightly. It was warmer there. That was where I spent that day and where I spent most of the next days too, for as Monika said, "When the rain stops it will be better upstairs, not such a refrigerator! I wouldn't want you to catch cold. Better stay close to the stove." If the message in her words hadn't stopped me from entering the studio, the closed door would.

I sketched the tile stove, and I sketched the pot of tea in front of me and the clock and the settee, and then I put my pen down. Outside the rain lashed against the house, and from time to time there was even thunder. I had brought only one book to read because I thought, like last year, I wouldn't have time. It was a novel by Erica Jong that my mother had pressed on me. "It's very avant-garde," she told me. "I think you'll like it." I read it the first day and then turned to the musty-smelling books on the shelves in the parlor. Most of them were in Swedish or another Scandinavian language, many leather-bound and from the turn of the century. Others had been published in the middle of this century. I imagined Uncle Edvard holed up here through the dark winters, loathing himself for not writing, hating his soon-to-be ex-wife and venting his ire on all the hopeful, timid writers of his time, those novelists who would be forgotten anyway, who now *were* forgotten, even without the help of his savaging. Uncle Edvard was probably forgotten too: "A minor critic of the mid century."

On the shelves were also some Norwegian 19th-century novels, from a time when literate people were more likely to read other Scandinavian languages. Here was a novel by Kitty's brother Alexander Kielland about a merchant family on the west coast. Here was Christian Krohg's *Albertine,* which had created such a scandal when it appeared. I had never read it but had heard about it; it was the story of a woman of the streets, like Zola's *Nana.* I remembered that the parents of the daughters Krohg taught painting to had removed their girls from class after the book came out.

Every evening Monika and I ate dinner together as usual, but conversation was often a little strained. She would say, "You must be so bored here. If only the rain would stop," and I would say, "Oh, I'm not bored at all. The cold is a relief after how how it was in Minnesota." I had thought this would be a time when the two of us could catch up on all the details that were lost in the letters, but whenever I tried to get more specific about her life, she changed the subject. The only thing I heard a great deal about was the village in Greece where she had stayed. I kept expecting that she would ask me more about how I'd passed the last year, but she did not. She would listen politely as I talked about my problems with my chairman over how many women to include in the course or about my growing involvement with *Demeter,* but she did not ask many questions.

After a few evenings I'd noticed that we didn't seem to be drinking wine with dinner this visit and had attributed it to Monika's new frugality. Wine was expensive in Sweden, and she'd probably gone through the case she'd bought from Germany at the beginning of the summer. So at a cost of something like $20 at the current exchange rate, I bought a bottle of ordinary French table wine from the little bar down at the harbor.

I told Monika I would make dinner that evening, and when I heard her coming downstairs I poured two glasses and gave her once. "To better weather!" I said, toasting. She toasted too. "I guess I hadn't noticed the weather today, isn't that awful? I must be getting used to it," she said, sipped at her drink, and then put it down. She was wearing, as usual, her long heavy sweater, with a scarf tied around her neck, and her hair pulled back. It was strange always to see her so bundled up, when last year she had been so brown and naked.

"I hope I haven't broken your solitude," I said. I meant it to be jocular and easy and was embarrassed when she considered it carefully.

"That is an odd English expression. Can solitude be broken? I don't see why I shouldn't keep my solitude whole and unharmed." She smiled. "Have I broken yours?"

"Yes. But in a good way. I was...sort of lonely this summer...before I arrived here."

She didn't respond immediately. Then she said, "I was often lonely over the last year. It was that more than anything that made me accept Sara's invitation to Greece. There was something about my life I was starting to hate." She took a tiny sip of wine. "Since coming back I have felt much better."

"Because now your art comes first."

"My art has always come first, I just couldn't do it as much as I wanted. No, it's more that at the moment I do not feel that my life is, what's the word? Useless."

I said, "There were times, when I didn't hear from you for a long time, that I thought I might never hear from you again. In a month or two so much can happen in a person's life."

"That's very true."

I needed to make sure she understood. I looked at her earnestly, an earnestness helped by two or three glasses of wine. "But it would be a terrible thing for me if we lost touch."

She reached over and patted my hand. "For me too," she said. "Writing you those letters, having a chance to put into words what I felt about my sense of isolation from people. It was really that, I think, that drove me to decide if I could change that and how."

I knew that Monika was telling me something important, but I couldn't quite ascertain if it had to do with me. I was still nervous that she might deliver some unwanted piece of news. "You didn't fall in love with anyone in Greece, did you?" I said, again trying for a light, a joking tone, and failing utterly.

She looked disappointed. "I don't think I believe in love anymore, not in the old way."

"Not in the old way?" I repeated. The old awful heterosexual way?

"There are other ways to change your life than to fall in love," she told me, getting up and beginning to clear the table.

I finished off my glass of wine and thought that over. I didn't know any.

The next morning I woke with a slight headache and an unfamiliar sensation on my face: sunshine. I looked out the window; the sea was calm, blue as a silk dress. The rocks were scoured gray and sparkling. I opened the window and breathed deep. Salt freshness and nothing on the horizon but more dazzling blue.

It was early, not yet 7. I put on my bathing suit; a dip in the salt water would clear my fuzzy head. I picked my way from memory to the two pools and when I arrived, Monika's head was just visible, seal-like, on the surface of the deeper pool.

"We had the same idea," I called and, daring, stripped off my suit. I felt that I could take it, however cold it was.

"Jump in," she invited. "But I warn you, it's freezing. I think I'm going to get out."

By the laughing way she said it, I knew that all the awkwardness of the past few days was over, and that now we would begin to enjoy ourselves as we had last summer.

"I'll wait a minute to see how blue you are," I said, and watched in pleasure as Monika began to pull herself up the ladder. First came the smooth brown arms and shoulders, then the high breasts with nipples shrunk to tiny brown bugs, breasts that looked fuller than I remembered them. I loved how Monika was so unself-conscious about her body in the nude. She saw me watching her and seemed to hesitate. I looked away—perhaps my eyes were too avidly on her—and then quickly back. She was standing just the way I remembered, brown in the sunlight, droplets of salt water beading her skin like pearls.

The only thing that was different was her stomach. My sister had gotten pregnant this spring and looked about the same.

"I was going to tell you," she said, coming over to me and drying off.

I had wrapped my towel around me and was huddled small and shocked at the edge of the pool.

"It's a big change in my life, but I didn't want...I don't want you to take it the wrong way."

The air felt so thin and fresh that it was almost hard to breathe. Monika sat down close to me and put her arm around me, the first time she had touched me since I came. Her body was very cold. I didn't dare touch her. My feelings were in an uproar.

"The father's name is Georgiou," she said after a while. "He lives in Athens most of the year and works as a taxi driver. He happened to be on the island where we went this spring, visiting his parents. He is a person I liked very much. He is full of life."

"You'll be living with Georgiou then when you go there?"

"Oh, no," said Monika. "He lives in Athens. It was just by coincidence he was there in May. Usually he spends the summers there, but he came early this year."

"Does he know about the baby?"

"I only found out when I came back to Germany. I lost his address."

"But won't his relatives guess…?"

"It may become known," she said mysteriously.

I saw suddenly how she might imagine it: sunny island months in Greece, Monika free to paint in her studio, the grandparents taking care of the baby, the father safely in Athens where he could put no claim on her. Maybe it wasn't as bad as I thought. I let myself lean against her,

"May I touch it?"

"Yes," she said, smiling.

I let my hand stroke her belly, feel her skin, warming now in the sun.

"It's not kicking or anything yet,"she said. "But I have been to the doctor on the mainland and everything is fine. It's about four months."

"If it's a girl, will you call her Anne?"

"No, I'll call her Sara, after my cousin." But she placed her hand on mine as I continued to stroke lightly around her belly.

"What does your family say?"

"They would be horrified if they knew. But we haven't spoken since before I went away. The Swedish side is far more forgiving. There are many single mothers in Sweden. Another reason for leaving Cologne."

It was hard to stop my hand from stroking lower or higher. My legs felt weak. "I never imagined what was under that huge sweater. Monika, I'm so pleased for you."

She hugged me closer. "And here I was afraid to tell you."

"Don't ever be afraid to tell me anything."

"And you don't be afraid either," she said.

"I won't," I lied.

The weather continued fine for several more days. It was not hot as it had been last year, but it was sunny. We worked in the garden in the afternoons, or sunbathed. Monika openly read a book on natural childbirth. She was expecting the baby in January. She would stay on the island through September and then go to Stockholm for the remaining months. She wanted to have the baby in Sweden, where the maternity care was good. I agreed with her plans and, though I didn't say anything, included myself in them. Staying in Sweden appealed to me. It was different than going to Germany. I was sure I could get some sort of teaching job here, or at the very least a research grant. I could expand my subject matter to include the neglected Swedish women painters of the 19th century.

Now that it was sunny, Monika's studio door stayed open and, although she never really did clear off a place for me, I took the opportunity to come in and draw her. She didn't seem to mind, in fact she was rather proud of the growing fullness of her body. Her arms and legs remained thin, of course, but overall there was a slightly flushed, swollen look, both silky and tight. A very gentle second chin was developing, and the small hump at the base of her neck was just a little more pronounced. I charted each change from last year with great tenderness on the page.

Thus the first week of my visit passed. Strained and then idyllic and then, as the wind came up one day and we had to go back indoors, strained again. I wanted to keep our happy mood and went down to purchase another expensively cheap bottle of wine. She didn't drink much but I did. After two glasses I found myself telling her, "You know I love to hear everything about your trip to Greece and your plans, Monika, but sometimes I feel like we always talk about your life. I feel like you never ask me anything about *my* life."

"I believed we both have shared a lot about ourselves. In our letters especially."

"About our inner lives, maybe. But not about our relationships."

"Oh, that's just gossip, social gossip."

"No, it's not. It's part of me. If you want to know me, then you need to know things about me."

"It's not what I need to know. It's what you want to tell me. What do you want to tell me, Anne?"

I told her about Jennifer, one of my professors in grad school. About gradually realizing that I liked spending time talking with her better than with any men I knew. About slowly realizing that she wanted more than friendship. Realizing that I wanted it too. I didn't go into the details of being lovers with Jennifer—the enormous awful secrecy because she was a professor and I was a student, because her family didn't know (though I was not the first student she'd been involved with) and thought that she was still seeing her old boyfriend—nor the way it had ended: painfully, with her coldly cutting me in the hallway after a misunderstanding, a misunderstanding she'd created. I simply told Monika we'd come to a parting of the ways when I was hired to teach in Minnesota.

Monika hadn't said anything, so I told her about going to teach in the small town in Minnesota, so much like the place I'd grown up in. I told her about my realization that none of the men people kept introducing me to were right, and that my lack of interest meant more than lack of interest. I told her about Lois and Mary Anne and Debbie. I talked for quite a long time before Monika interrupted.

"Is the point of all this to tell me you're a lesbian?" she asked. "Because if so, I already know."

"You know?"

"I'm not a fool."

"And it's all right with you?"

"Why should it matter if it's all right with me? It's your life. I have known lesbians before," she added. "My cousin Sara, in fact, is bisexual."

"But have you ever, yourself, I mean...?"

"It's not something I feel opposed to. I've just not thought about it."

I didn't believe her; I believed she'd thought about it and had come to no conclusion except that it frightened her.

"But I don't think that what I feel is completely one-sided. Is it?"

"Don't tell me what you feel. It's really better."

"You didn't answer my question."

"It's not a question I can answer."

I should have backed off then or been softer or more mysterious. But the wine had done its work. I heard an awful wheedling tone come into my voice. "Don't you want to find out who you really are?"

"I know who I really am."

"You don't."

"Anne, are you drunk?"

"Yes, but it's your fault. You keep pouring me wine and not drinking any yourself."

"I can't drink now. I'm just polite."

"I don't want anything from you. I just want...to love you. I'm sorry."

"Anne," she got up and moved away from me, "let's leave it for now, all right?"

The next day it rained, and the two days after. The second week of my stay was drawing to a close. There were no bike rides and little sunbathing because of the weather. Monika worked most days in her studio. Very occasionally I worked with her and drew her figure in a dozen poses. Other days, catching a tone in her voice or seeing her door closed, I stayed downstairs by the coal fire. I began to read a novel by the 19th-century Norwegian writer Amalie Skram. *Professor Hieronymus* was the story of a woman painter called Else who couldn't paint and couldn't sleep and ended up going to a mental institution thinking she was going to rest, but instead she was trapped there, diagnosed as hopelessly insane by the doctor in charge.

I was waiting for a little time to pass since my declaration of love. I tried to act cheerful and patient, to keep the discussion on art and literature and away from personal subjects. I thought Monika and I were doing pretty well, but one night, she asked me over dinner, "How long do you think of staying? When is your conference in Norway?"

I couldn't tell her that the seminar was in October. I said, "When would you like me to leave?"

"It's not that. I've liked having you here, only…"

"Only now you'd like to be alone?"

"I'm not as neurotic as you think I am," said Monika with a smile. "I'm simply selfish when it comes down to it. Selfish about my time, like all artists. You are selfish too, if you could admit it."

"I'll leave tomorrow," I said, ignoring all that. "With the weather so bad, it really hasn't been much of a vacation."

"Where will you go?"

"Norway, probably. I have friends there. I can always do some research." I started out confidently, but ended a little woe-begonely. I didn't have the money it would take to live in Norway for any length of time; I would have to go back to Minnesota. I had to go back there anyway, to start teaching after Labor Day.

"You don't have to leave so soon."

"But if my presence annoys you..."

"How can I explain? It's not your presence in particular. You know that I am fond of you. It's anybody's presence when I'm working, I suppose. Having to be conscious of someone else around."

"What will you do when you have a child around all day and night?"

"Believe me, I sometimes worry. But I hope—because the baby will be part of me—that I can somehow manage."

"You could pretend that I'm your big baby," I said, only

partly joking. "You could practice on me."

Monika laughed, and the subject was dropped. I did not leave for Norway, and the next day the weather was fine. We took the afternoon off and went to Marstrand, a charming, pricey island in the archipelago, where we had a late lunch in an outdoor café overlooking a harbor full of yachts.

More and more often our conversations tended to go like this: A few truths were said, a threat was made, reassurances were offered, and the whole thing was dropped until the next time. In my happier moments I believed that Monika was getting more used to me and that my persistence was paying off. Persistence in service of what goal, I never really asked myself. Did I want her to fall in love with me and, if so, what did I imagine would be the result of a such a love? Was I prepared to throw up everything at home to move here and take care of Monika's baby so she could paint? Did I think that I could somehow pursue my academic career while living on a Swedish island? And what about this whole Greek connection? What if Georgiou the father came back into the picture? What if Monika wanted him to?

One dull and misty morning I found myself writing a letter to Evie. I wrote about Monika being pregnant and my desire for her, a desire that had no basis and no future. I wrote about being on this island in bad weather and how it made me feel claustrophobic. I wrote about my inability to do the drawing that I'd hoped for because the drawing I wanted to do was all of Monika's body and I couldn't get near enough to do it.

"If she would only tell me to leave," I wrote. "It would be

better. But she doesn't tell me, and I can't force myself. It is the most abasing thing I know, to love someone and not to be loved back. And to keep hoping that the sun will come out again and she will take off that sweater and hold me close. I don't want anything more than to lie next to her. I wouldn't even do anything."

By the time I got to this part of the letter I knew that I would never send it. I shoved it into my rucksack instead, and eventually it made its way into the box of sketchbooks at the bottom of a box, buried in the studio. When I read it now I feel almost a voyeur of my own longing and pain, but less embarrassed than I could be. Instead I marvel at how strongly I felt and at my insistence that to love and not be loved back was abasing.

I wrote all my pain out to Evie without thinking of who Evie was to receive it and what she'd think. I started writing to Evie and ending up writing to myself. And then I put the letter away. That afternoon the clouds suddenly blew away, in the space of 15 minutes, and Monika came downstairs in shorts and a big T-shirt, with her hair in a shiny ponytail, "Quick, quick. Let's get the bikes and catch the ferry in 20 minutes. I have been dying for lack of exercise. We won't bother about a picnic, we'll find some food on the way. Quick, quick."

I leaped to follow her out the door, forgetting to take money, sunscreen, or a sweater. We grabbed the bikes and trundled them as fast as we could down the hill, arriving at the dock just in time to meet the ferry coming in. Half an hour later we were on an island where I had not been and cycling up a hill. Monika had not been here in some time, but she remembered a beach with white sand and a kiosk nearby where we could get a sandwich or hot dog. It was sunny, even hot, when we started out, and I fiercely missed my sunscreen. I could practically hear the skin on my shoulders crisping up. But by the time we reached the turnoff to the beach Monika remembered, the clouds had moved in again, as fast as they had left.

The beach was long and sandy, but deserted. The kiosk, and there had been one, was boarded up. Near it was a small stand of beech trees, rustling in the thin hard breeze.

"Maybe we should go back," I suggested.

"Oh, no," said Monika, stripping off her clothes, leaving them where they fell, and running for the water. "I'm dying for a swim."

Against my better judgment, for we had no towels and the sky was threatening, I took off all my clothes too, feeling small and defenseless. Particles of sand stung my skin as I walked toward the water. I couldn't bring myself to go in any deeper than to my knees. The waves sloshed up against my calves and up my thighs, leaving a chill afterward. Monika was already 50 feet away from me down the beach. The current was pulling her parallel to the shore. I felt the same dragging at my legs, but unlike Monika, who let herself be carried, floating on her back with her feet sticking up, I tried to keep standing still, to hold my ground. The weight and force of the sea felt enormous. It wasn't the Atlantic, but the Atlantic was out there behind this water and backing it up with all its huge power. I shouted to Monika, something meant to sound cheerful—"This is the first time I've really understood what a current is"—but that sounded hysterical. Monika didn't hear, though, didn't even see that I'd opened my mouth.

I stood up to my waist in the freezing gray water and felt the hands of the sea pull me in Monika's direction. Why didn't I just follow? I felt the sand disappearing from under my feet, making craters in the sand beneath me, so that I staggered and had to keep finding my footing. After only a short while I looked up and realized that the bikes and our clothes were not where they should be. I too was being pulled against my will.

Then the storm moved in, cold and fast. It hit as we were still in the water. The rain beat down, icy hard drops; the sea pulled harder at my legs. "Monika," I shouted, but she was hardly visible, and the wind, in any case, carried away my words. Every step back to the beach was an effort. When I finally got out, I stood shivering under the beech trees. Our clothes on the sand were soaked. I felt like a naked castaway.

But the storm passed as suddenly as it started. Monika came strolling up the beach just as the sun burst out. She stretched and laid her clothes out to dry. "That felt so wonderful," she said jubilantly. "Wasn't that wonderful?"

Her nakedness was a torment to me even as I loved how easy she was with her body. She sat cross-legged on the damp sand and ran her fingers through her hair and shook it out.

I began to tell her about thunderstorms in the Midwest, which didn't seem to blow in from anywhere as these sea storms did, but which bred, it seemed, on themselves, intensifying out of nothing, like a fist that derives its power from clenching. I told her about thunder and lightning on the lake in Minnesota, and about *The Four-Story Mistake.* I told her about looking for the secret room by pressing one knot after the next, three summers in a row. I told her what I had never told anybody else, how after I had forgotten all about the secret room I had rediscovered the attic at 12 and 13 with Nancy. "We used to go there on hot, rainy summer days and take off our clothes and without speaking rub up against each other until we each had an orgasm. We didn't stop because anyone found out, but because Nancy got a boyfriend. We've never spoken of it, and I can't tell her how it was the beginning for me, not something meaningless or shameful."

"It's not shameful," said Monika. "Other girls do it. I did it too."

"With Sara?"

"With Sara. Only in our case, she was the one who went further with it."

"You could go further. I know you could."

"Yes, I could, you're right," Monika said, but she drew up her knees so that her belly was hidden. "But what good would that do you or me? Yes, we could make love. We could have made love last year and all this month, but what would be the use? You would always want more, and I could never give you more. I don't want anyone close to me like that. I don't want to have a lover making demands on me that I can't live up to."

"I don't want more. I mean, I do, I want whatever you can give, but not an ounce more, not if you don't want it."

"Don't make it so hard, Anne. Please try to understand."

I thought I would die if she didn't unfold her knees, didn't stop looking at me with pity and not desire. "Only what you want. Only as far as you want."

"And if I want nothing?"

"You slept with some Greek guy without caring. Can't you sleep with me? Would it be so awful?"

"It's not because I would find it awful or shameful. I don't think that way."

"You'd rather have a baby than a lover because you can control a baby better," I said angrily.

"I don't think I will be able to control my love for a baby at all. That's why I wanted a child."

"But you said you didn't want a lover making demands."

"You don't understand anything. A lover I can say no to—a lover I can hurt, I *will* hurt. But a baby—I would never turn my back on a baby."

The way her parents had turned their backs on her, the way she would want to make up for.

I felt the first drops spatter against my forehead and realized that the sky had changed again. This time it was not a wild brief storm, but turned into a steady dull downpour that followed us all the way back to the ferry, a half hour away.

We had to wait an hour for it to arrive. Monika was shivering uncontrollably by then, and her breaths came in wheezy gasps.

During the two times I'd stayed on the island, I had become aware that Monika neither had friends nor wanted them here. I'd asked her once or twice what she would do in an emergency, who would help her. "I'd call Sara," she'd said.

"No, seriously," I'd said. "Which neighbor would you ask?"

"I always find it hard to ask for help," she'd finally said. "The family has always stayed a little apart, not just me. First it was because they were bourgeois people from Göteborg and most of the people here were fishermen, and then there was my Uncle Edvard—he refused to talk to anybody—and now there's me, withdrawn by nature. I don't really know anyone here."

Back at the house, I put Monika on the sofa by the coal stove and went to find her inhaler and asthma medication in the bathroom. At that point she could still talk, though only with great effort. Her forehead was warm, but her hands and feet were icy. While she sucked on the inhaler and took the medication, I found towels and blankets and dried her off and wrapped her up well. I managed to get some water and then tea down her before letting her lie back, gasping. I expected that she would gradually relax and begin to breathe normally, as she did last year. All thoughts of love and sexual need seemed driven from my mind. I saw her fall into a feverish slumber and heard her breathing slow, but she still seemed chilled. I lay down next to her on the sofa to warm her, and within minutes I was asleep too.

I had a horrible dream. I was touching Nan in the attic when gradually I realized that she was pregnant, all swollen and sweating. I thought she was going to give birth, but it was too early; she was miscarrying, in a pool of blood and greenish fluid. The baby fell out, dead, on to the floor. It was perfectly formed, little shell-like hands, open eyes.

When I woke it seemed very dark in the room, though I could see it was still light outside. Monika was laboring to breathe. Her eyes seemed to be popping from her head in panic. I gave her the inhaler, which seemed hardly to help. She couldn't get her breath enough to even speak. I could see fear in her green eyes.

And I began to panic too. I was still in the grip of the dream and thought that she might be miscarrying as well as having an asthma attack. I forced myself not to show my fear, though, but to say very quietly, "Monika, I'm going to call Sara and ask what to do, if that's all right with you."

She nodded, but couldn't help me find the phone number. I pawed through stacks of papers on the secretary, finding the Belgian seashell chocolates in their midst, until I located a battered address book. Sara Lundgren's name was there, thank God. I dialed the number in Stockholm.

A woman's voice answered on the second ring. I could see the clock in the kitchen. It was about 9. The wind blew hard outside. It wasn't dark, though it seemed as if it should be.

"My name is Anne, a friend of Monika's. I'm here with her on the island. She's having trouble breathing, she can't talk. What should I do?"

"She can't speak herself to me?"

"She can hardly get her breath."

"You've tried the medication? The inhaler?"

"They don't help."

"Here is what you must do. Go to the blue house below ours. Tell Mr. Andersson he must take Monika to the hospital in his boat. No, tell him he must call the ambulance to wait at the dock of the mainland. Tell him you talked with me. I will call the hospital. They know her."

"This has happened before?"

"Do everything I've told you. Do it right now. It won't get better."

We hung up. Sara's calmness had infected me. I went outside, to the blue house I had passed several times a day last year and this. Monika had never told me the name of the older couple who lived there. As briskly as I could, I told them in English what was necessary, thinking, as I said it aloud, that it was a larger undertaking than Sara had suggested. But the Anderssons had lived on the island a long time, and there had been other emergencies. Mr. Andersson put on a slicker and gave one to me; he followed me up to the house and took Monika in his arms and brought her down through the houses to the harbor. It was an old fishing boat that he had. He placed her down below in the cabin and started the boat. All this time the rain was coming down and the wind was blowing and yet it wasn't dark, only an eerie gray. The crossing took only ten minutes and at the other end an ambulance was waiting. They would not let me go with her, and Andersson took me back. It was, I think now, the last time I saw Monika.

I don't remember much about that evening; everything was storm and adrenaline and fear and gray. I only remember Monika's hot skin and her fevered, gasping breathing, and how being sick made her seem so young. When I lay down beside her in the cabin below, it was like lying next to a child. My sexual desire had left me. I only wanted her to live.

The last week of my stay on the island passed peacefully, though not as I would have imagined, for Monika did not return. She was in the hospital for several days and then, without telling me, she flew to Stockholm.

I received a phone call from Sara one evening to tell me that Monika was with her. Given the asthma that seemed to have been caused by overexertion, a chill, and perhaps by "stress," the doctors did not think it wise for her to return to the island. "She was going to come here to Stockholm in September anyway, for the baby's sake, so this is just a little earlier. She says please to stay as long as you like there, though. When you leave just give the keys to the Anderssons. I will try to get there before the cold weather begins, to close things up for the season."

Sara's voice was steady, kind, and somehow final. It was as if we hadn't been through a crisis together, as if I were totally outside the family circle and had no claim on Monika at all. And it was true: I had no claim. I couldn't even manage to ask how Monika was—my shock at realizing she didn't want to speak with me was so great. I said something mechanical about giving the keys to the Anderssons and then blurted out, "I didn't mean to cause her stress."

"I know you didn't," said Sara in the same kind but distant way. "It's only how she is. She runs when she gets too close."

I could have left immediately, but I didn't. I stayed on three more days. During that time I went through a range of emotions, from rage at how she'd treated me—I had saved her life, after all—to shame that I had driven Monika out of her own home to self-pity that she had not loved me back. Obsessively I went over our last day together. It had been her idea to go on the bike ride. And then she had as much as told me that she had thought of, had even wanted to make love with me and couldn't. And then I had taken care of her. I had held her close to warm her. I had found out what to do in a strange country and had done it. I had huddled with her on a stormy sea telling her to breathe. And she couldn't even say good-bye.

The weather was almost perfect that last week. Not hot as it had been last year, but golden with the romantic warm light of late summer, for it was by now the end of August. The first few days that I was waiting for Monika to return I did everything I had wanted to do this whole visit. I rose early and had tea in the garden. I took my sketchbook out and drew the sea; I threw myself into the salt ponds, I let the sea pound me. I spent hours in her atelier drawing shells. Evenings I sat outside and read.

The last three days I did the same things, with bereft determination.

The evening before I was to leave the phone rang.

"Oh, you're still there," Monika said, nervous.

"You said I could stay as long as I liked."

"Yes, of course, of course. How is the weather?"

"It's become beautiful since you left."

"Then I envy you. Here it's been gray and rainy. Have you been swimming?"

"Yes, and sitting in the garden and getting up in the morning and drawing. Just like we used to do."

"Oh, it's terrible. I just left my paintings there, I was in such a hurry. You know the doctors *threatened* me. They said, 'Don't you dare go somewhere without a hospital nearby.' Such nonsense. I have been completely fine for days."

"Then come back. Everything is here."

"I don't like to be sick, for people to think I'm sick," she said, almost petulantly. "And this baby—now I have to worry about its health too."

"Come back," I said. "Just to see the wonderful August light. Just to swim a few more times."

"I don't dare," she said. "Sara has been lecturing me about all sorts of things. Health. Motherhood. My responsibilities."

"She's a good friend to you."

"She saves me from myself sometimes. She understands how afraid I get."

"She's a good friend," I repeated dully.

Monika paused and then said, in a small voice, "It seems unlikely that we'll see each other again—I mean, this year."

"Yes," I said.

"Perhaps we'll write." She sounded uncertain.

"Perhaps."

"You write me first. Then I'll answer."

"Perhaps," I said again, and then, "I'd better go and pack now. Thanks for calling."

It was the last time that we spoke. After we hung up I was restless. It was only 7 and I had the whole evening to get through. I went to the sea, but it was too big for me. I thought about throwing myself in the salt ponds, but I didn't want to get wet and think of Monika. I sat on the rocks watching the sun, but the sky had a lonely look and the ocean air was too soft and sad. I wandered down to the harbor feeling displaced, aching. The pleasure boaters had doggedly stuck out the weather and were now rewarded with a golden evening in which to sit on their boats and eat dinner, drink, and play cards.

Thanks to Monika I now knew that what I felt looking at them was piercing loneliness.

On the way back up the hill I ran into Mr. and Mrs. Andersson. They reminded me of some relatives on my father's side. I couldn't imagine how Monika had managed to avoid talking to them for six years. They stopped and asked me, the friendly sweet American girl, about Monika, and I said that she wouldn't be coming back this summer.

"She always kept to herself. Like her Uncle Edvard," they said. "You're the only visitor we can remember her ever having here."

I went back to the yellow house, let myself in, and went upstairs to pack. Why me? Why had Monica chosen me to come here?

I went into her studio and opened the windows. The long drapes blew in. The wind was colder, sharper now, but the light still stayed. It would stay for two hours yet. I decided to sit there until sunset, and I did. I watched how the walls were finally washed with delicate light, gold and pink and peach, just like the inside of a shell.

IV. Self-portrait

The number of women artists who painted portraits in the 18th and 19th centuries was considerable, and the women painters in Norway during the period 1850–1900 were among that group. Most of the portraits were painted for clients and were meant to flatter and to show status. These women subjects of the leisure class are posed to look soft and feminine, wearing fine dress, surrounded by objects of luxury. In general the women in these portraits seem to lack personality; the emphasis tends to be on their dress and hair, the furniture and baubles that surround them. There are exceptions, however: a portrait of the novelist Amalie Skram by Leis Schelderup, for instance. The portrait of Kitty Kielland by Harriet Backer makes Kitty look frighteningly forceful, stern and dark.

The self-portraits that these artists painted, like the self-portraits women have often done, are quite different from their portraits of other women. I have looked at most of the Norwegian women painters' pictures of themselves. I was not the first to note, though I like to imagine I would have seen it too, that to a one these self-portraits are direct, confident, quizzical, strong, unflattering, searching. They do not seem afraid to look straight at themselves and see what is under the beauty or lack of beauty. In fact, in terms of the way these artists look at themselves, I would not even use the word beauty. All of them seem to ask the question, Who am I? and in some way try to answer it.

Evie Parkins met me at the airport on my return from Sweden, and within a week we were a couple. Things seemed to happen with a kind of fatalistic rapidity and without my thinking too deeply. It was almost as if I had decided months ago or in my sleep what I would do if Monika refused to fall in love with me.

I remember that it pleased me, although it hurt too, to say yes to Evie when she asked if I wanted her, if I loved her. It pleased me to give someone back the love she desired so much, and that's why it hurt too. With Evie, except for the first few times we made love, when I was still desperately trying to find someone else in her, there was no deep desire, no all-consuming passion. I felt only a kind of gratitude, and then a dull, buried anger over being so adored. After a short while, though, Evie became familiar to me: blond and short as I was, snub-nosed, opinionated in a changeable sort of way. The only thing she never changed her mind about was me. No one was ever so loyal. Even today, when I bump into her I'm uncomfortably reminded (does she remind me?) that if I hadn't run off with Beth, the two of us might still be together.

Before classes started in the fall I had already moved to Minneapolis. Evie and I found a large old house to rent and invited Lisa and Laura, new members of the journal collective, to move in with us. I commuted every day, but my heart wasn't in teaching there any longer. I grew more involved with *Demeter* and stayed up late talking and arguing with Evie and our roommates about the direction it should go. I was, meanwhile, the only one who had a regular and decently paid job, so I usually made up the shortfall between the printers' bills and postage and what money we collected from subscriptions and grants. We were a collective and everyone had her say, but the work—and the responsibility—was never shared equally. Evie remained the organizer, and much of what she organized was me. Lisa and Laura had strong opinions that informed all our work; they drew other collective members in and pushed them out again. We lived together in our own version of a feminist artistic milieu and gradually formed a network of like-minded women around us.

Somewhere during this first year of living with Evie and the others, although I had good intentions, I stopped taking art classes or doing any drawing. I came up for tenure and was denied it. It was one thing to write about 19th-century women's art and deliver papers on Harriet Backer and Kitty Kielland at academic conferences; it was another entirely to curate a show of all-lesbian work in Minneapolis and to get my name in the paper over it. After the hostility that surfaced during the tenure fight and the lack of strong support from colleagues I had considered friends, I felt I could no longer each there and gave up my job, partly at Evie's urging. She told me I could find a job easily in Minneapolis or St. Paul.

I spent a year on unemployment before the university finally hired me, and for someone like me, in school since the age of five and driven by a fierce Protestant work ethic, this was a terrible thing. The family had seen my name in the paper in connection with the lesbian art exhibit, and while I had only been called a "respected feminist art historian," the more clever members put this fact together with the knowledge that I had neither a boyfriend nor husband and that I had quit my job and gone to live in an urban center with a bunch of girls. I never did come out properly, the way I had, in moments of sentimentality, imagined that I would. My mother said later she had suspected for some years, and she mentioned the time I came home at Christmas from graduate school and kept sitting by the phone waiting for a call from "one of my professors."

"I wasn't going to ask you and embarrass you," said my mother when, just recently, we sat down and talked about what had happened. "I'm more used to it now," she apologized. "It's on television and everything. And you know we all like Beth."

"Except Nan."

"Well, Nan wouldn't, would she, now that she's been saved and all."

We looked at each other and I thought, *She knows about me and Nan somehow. She's always known about me.*

"Beth is a wonderful person," my mother said more firmly. "She's the right one for you."

I never wrote to Monika again. In the beginning, just after returning from Sweden, I meant to write. I was going to tell her about Evie, tell her there was someone who loved me very much. I meant to give Monika my new address. I meant to ask her how she was and where she was. I meant to continue on paper a kind of dialogue about the requirements of a woman artist, to argue against solitude and for community, for political involvement and against individual ego.

I got as far as scribbling, "Dear Monika, Thank you for..." before putting down my pen.

She didn't care what I thought. She had never cared. But when January came every year I wondered what she was doing to celebrate her baby's birthday.

In this period this was no lack of political support for me in my new lesbian family, my new feminist network. But after the drama of the tenure rejection wore off, there wasn't much active support either. I had a Ph.D., what was I complaining about? *They* had to work as waitresses and typesetters. I hid the pain of not teaching by throwing myself into *Demeter,* becoming the unpaid office person, the design and layout worker (I use person and worker to mean manager here; we did not use terms like director and supervisor). I thought I had a role to play at the journal as a feminist art historian, but soon I came to understand that, far from being considered an expert in the area of women's art, I was, in fact, highly suspect because of my academic credentials. It seemed clear to Lisa and Laura in particular that, because of my research and writing on Kitty Kielland and Harriet Backer, my emphasis on their lives and paintings, I still believed in autonomous individualism. That is, the artist as a solitary individual who created out of her own imagination, not the artist as cultural worker who created out of shared communal values.

Although Evie had begun *Demeter* as a literary and aesthetic experiment (an origin she later felt forced to deny) the other women in the *Demeter* collective were less interested in the individual and her imagination than in the concept of community. At first I thought I knew what they meant by *community* or *the community* (as if there were only one), and it gave me a warm, solid feeling (the same feeling I thought about expressing to Monika in a forceful letter) when I heard or used the word. After so many years of being excluded (and this also meant years when I had pretended I was included because I was closeted) to now be swept up in a larger group of women felt like heaven at first. I took any criticism of my previous views about art and artists to be more or less true, and I tried to correct my outworn, retrograde thinking.

At that time, if I had listed the conditions that made possible the artistic life of the female cultural worker, I would have written:

Community

Money

Emotional support

But gradually, as the years wore on, I began to sense that *community,* at least in our circle, was a code word for a certain starchily correct part of the lesbian subculture. Which was less like a community than a self-policing entity with subtle distinctions, fierce angers, and long memories. It was perhaps the third year of my involvement with Evie and *Demeter* that I began to have problems with my chosen community, though it would also be fair to say that it began to have problems with me.

Demeter had, since its inception, been accused of various sins and omissions, most of which it was guilty of. It was too middle-class; it was not lesbian enough at first, and then it was too lesbian. It had avoided controversy, it had been elitist, but now it went out of its way to stir up divisiveness and be provocative. The main thing it was, though, and there no disputing this, was far too white. Finally after various breast-beating collective meetings, it was decided that the next issue would be a multicultural one. There would be guest editors, who would hopefully become collective members. An exploratory meeting was held, which was pretty much a fiasco. I don't quite recall all the details, but in her nervous desire not to make any mistakes, Laura said something unforgivably racist. Lisa tried to cover up for her, Evie tried to apologize for her, and I sat dumbly in shame and frustration at being a part of this at all—none of which were useful responses.

It was at this gathering that Beth and I saw each other for the first time. Actually I think I saw her back as she got up and left the room. She later remembered me as one of those sorry-assed white women. But some months later, as *Demeter* was in the recriminatory throes of its last issue, and poor Evie, knowing the impossibility of pleasing everyone and feeling ill-used and responsible on account of being the founder of this journal, had fled to California to visit a cousin, I ran into Beth at a party.

It was her eyes that struck me first. They were large and green, a little darker than Monika's and set against skin the color of warm oak. Nothing else was physically like Monika—Beth is husky, flat-chested, big-hipped, with an almost shaved head—but for an instant I was reminded of another party, five years before this summer, at an Oslo gallery.

There were other funny similarities. Beth taught kids as well as old and homeless people. She'd grown up outside Stuttgart, daughter of a German woman and a black soldier, who had later divorced. She had gone to high school in Germany and then come to Chicago to visit her father's side of the family. She was still here 15 years later. She had a faint but recognizable German accent.

"I know someone from Cologne," I found myself saying. "I used to anyway." And then I asked Beth about her work. Her enthusiasm charmed me. It was so open and joyous, so different from the way that Lisa and Laura and even Evie talked about their "day jobs," which were so oppressive, and their "cultural work," which placed tremendous burdens of doing right on their tender shoulders. Beth had a day job, which was teaching art, and her own art, but somehow there was no separation between them, only a kind of flowing back and forth. If she was making murals with kids, she might make them at home too, on the garage wall. If she was teaching senior citizens to videotape each other telling their life stories, she might draw them as they talked.

"Could I see slides of your work sometime?" I wondered, still wearing the *Demeter* cap.

"Come and see the work itself," she said. "My kids are in the middle of a big mural project. I was thinking of stopping by after the party anyway to look at it. Come with me."

Half an hour later we were standing in front of a recreation building at a local park admiring a scene taken from the early days of Minnesota history.

"I wish I'd never grown up," I said. "I used to love working on these kinds of things at school."

"What's stopping you?" Beth said. It could have been challenging, but it felt kind. And then when I didn't say anything, she took my hand and began to move it in circles, so that I could feel a loosening of my wrist and elbow and shoulders. Of my heart, too.

"Just because you're an art historian," she said, smiling, "doesn't mean you should stop drawing pictures."

It was Beth who got me drawing again, and it's Beth who pushes me when I forget about it. "Let's go out to the studio," she says, the studio which is in the garage out back of our house. "Let's draw some pictures." Beth is always making art; I only work sporadically. I have periods when I work in a disciplined manner, times when, for instance, I take a class or decide to master a new medium or meet with friends in a critique group. Times when I carry a sketchbook everywhere and find myself recording what I see. At such times I can make myself believe that I am a serious artist, that I could have a show someday, that I have something to say, a particular vision.

Usually after a few weeks, sometimes a few months, this impulse leaves me. I used to feel embarrassed about this ebb and flow—grandiosity followed by humbleness and then stretches of silence and frustration. And then a kind of indifference that is perhaps partly willed forgetfulness, disguised with phrases about being too busy. Women like Beth, like Monika, they're the true artists. It never leaves them, this impulse to create. It fills their days and nights and takes them over. I can only marvel and persevere in my own up-and-down way.

Some of my graduate students are postmodernists and often write and speak in terms that, although I understand them intellectually, seem almost senseless sometimes. They speak disparagingly of paintings as cultural artifacts that have been privileged over other forms of art. To these students the artist is not a heroic figure who strives to make visual the inner workings of her soul; in fact, her intentions are less important than the ideologies she represents or that the viewer or critic may freely read into her work. Their papers are full of Foucault and Derrida, with quotations from Kristeva. They write of disruptions and interruptions. "Transgressive" is big this year, "subversion" last year. They are would-be academics who probably once loved to draw pictures, young people who speak of subverting the dominant paradigm, yet who would not think of doing what Beth does, going out into the world open-handed with her gifts to share them. Much better to sit in a classroom and critique what has been done before or to imagine what never can be done. Kitty and Harriet and their bourgeois easel paintings are of little interest to these students. Two old Norwegian spinsters, painting middle-class pictures of interiors, of women before an open window.

When I have enough of their talk, sometimes I'll say, "Go down to the art store and buy a pad of newsprint and a few pieces of charcoal. Sit for an hour and draw. Tell me how the chalk feels on the page gliding over the rough gray paper. Are you empty, afraid, peaceful, excited? What do the shapes mean to you? Why are the marks you make like no one else's? Do this an hour every day—if you can bear it—and then come back and tell me that the artist's intentions have no significance."

And then I try to do the same thing myself.

If I had painted my own self-portrait ten years ago, if I'd been honest enough to have painted it clearly, I would have painted a young woman with an untried, yearning look, soft at the edges, selfish but not ruthless, full of false modesty and utopian theories she was afraid to try out. I would have painted a woman with unlined skin, weak around the mouth, with eyes behind glasses that were curious but naive. I would have painted her with some sense of shame burned deeply into her brain for who she was and who she loved. I would have gotten beneath the exterior of that image I presented to the world and had presented since I was young: peppy, "go get 'em," problem-free. I would have tried to paint the girl who, the summers she was eight and nine and even ten, had methodically pressed every knot on a staircase wall, trying to find the secret room where she could be loved and yet herself, where she could be surrounded and yet alone.

I think Beth caught a little of that, the weakness, the yearning, the strength, the shame when she painted my portrait five years ago. She made me beautiful, though, because that's how her love sees me. Even today, she would paint me like that, though she would have to see more wrinkles and gray hair, less yearning, more strength. I would not paint myself that way. I do not see myself as beautiful. I neither can nor want to.

These are some of the things I've wondered about Monika Diechmann as the years have passed. How is her health? Was her labor hard and how has her baby—Sara if she's a girl—thrived? Did Monika go back to Greece the following spring and carry out her decision to divide her time between a Greek island and a Swedish one? Has she managed to carry out the plan she conceived of living solely for her art, a solitude broken only by the needs of her child?

I wonder, not if Monika is still painting, for I know she is, but just what she is painting. I feel a real curiosity about this. Has she gone more abstract or more figurative? Surely she can't be still painting shells and islands, but if she is, then what do those shells and rocks look like? Of course I would like to know about her career: whether, for instance, she has been able to support herself painting, or has gone back to teaching. One thing I feel I know for sure, she is not involved with a woman, the way I am with Beth, and I doubt that she came to love and live with a man, though it's possible. Perhaps it's just completely wrong, but I find it difficult, almost impossible, to imagine her anything but alone. Even though she has a child, I see her as independent and solitary. I find I envy her this.

I envy her not because I don't love Beth and don't love our life together. If she left me I would suffer terribly. Our life together is rich and full. She has opened my world with her spirit and generosity. But I envy Monika precisely because I love Beth enough to believe I couldn't live without her and would never want to leave what we have together. I envy Monika because, instead of the fertile, muddy waters of love, she has something else running in her veins, clearer, colder, fresher.

Why do we love the people whom we love? My parents I loved because they were my parents, my cousin Nan because she made me understand the power of a woman's body. I loved my first boyfriend because he hit more home runs than anybody our junior year, because I wanted to be normal and loving him proved I was. I loved Jennifer, my professor, because she created an air of desperation, mystery, and illicit passion around our rather conventional affair. Mary Lou I loved because she was 36 when I was 26 and because she knew everything about her Ford pickup there was to know. Debbie I loved when I was 28 because she spoke French so beautifully and always wore shoes that she'd bought in Paris. Lois I loved because she was prematurely gray and was, like me, a historian, and knew the peculiar lure of imagining oneself in the past. Evie I loved quite desperately the week I came back from Sweden and far less desperately the four years afterward. I loved her because she knew what she wanted from me and I could give it to her, or so I thought at first, not realizing what a difference there is between responding to another's passion and feeling passion oneself. Beth I love how I love my family (though my sister still gets on my nerves and Nan has become a fundamentalist Christian). I don't have to work at it; it's there like the sun coming up every morning, like the moon at night.

Now that I know what real love feels like, how it feels day in and out, it doesn't seem quite right to say I loved anybody before Beth, much less that I loved Monika Diechmann. It would probably be better to say, as Evie told me when I got back from the island, that I'd been the victim of an unhealthy obsession. Certainly Monika never loved me. If she had she would have written, wouldn't she?

This week I began to paint my portrait. I'd been thinking about it since I turned 40 and began to move into the second half of my life, to be neither young nor young-looking. Now I had the time, a whole summer off. I made a place for myself in the studio and got out the pastels. Living with a working artist has many benefits, including all the art supplies you need. Beth says I should work harder at my painting, and I always nod, for I do love it. But I am not ruthless, as Monika noted long ago. I am not driven to make art, as I am driven to do research, teach, and write. I draw and paint for pleasure and because it reminds me of some part of myself that I have always lost and found, over and over.

Still I wanted to do my own self-portrait. I wanted to see what I would see in my face and in my eyes. Perhaps it was also spurred by a letter I got this week from Germany. Beth has been there visiting her mother. The blue airmail letter with the pedestrian stamp on it took me back to another summer long ago, when I looked daily in my postbox for messages from Monika. There was little of Monika's abstract thinking in Beth's letter, and yet she wrote of enjoying the chance to travel on her own. She had been to Munich to look at pictures. She would be going to Paris next. It wasn't threatening to read that she was enjoying her solitude, for I was feeling that same enjoyment myself. Often enough I had worked with Beth in the studio and found great pleasure in it. I'd thought about Harriet and Kitty working together and alone and had realized, *Somehow I've managed it too, to find both love and solitude.* For me neither one could ever be enough. The knot I tried to find on the stairway to the attic finally responded to my touch: The door opened, and I found myself alone, in a house inhabited by my family.

I had decided to place myself at an easel, working in the studio. It was a convention I had always liked. Quickly I outlined my figure in jeans and a paint-stained white shirt. I painted the outlines of my face, turned toward the viewer. For some reason I felt moved to paint myself with glasses, though I usually wear contacts now, and with a serious expression. I worked on my face for two days before turning to the background. That's what sent me to the photo album again and to the letters. I even tried to find Monika's island off the coast of Sweden in an atlas. It was not visible, of course. But I did find the box of sketchbooks and the watercolors, far back in a closet, buried under boxes of more recent work. I dragged everything out into the light and looked at it. Not bad, not as bad as I had feared. I put many things in the background of my self-portrait, things that had once been important to me. On a table near the easel was a luminous conch, a piece of dark rock, a blue airmail letter postmarked Cologne, and a map of Sweden with a ferry schedule covering part of it. On the wall I painted in a small rendering of Oda Krohg's dreamy picture of a woman looking out a window, no, not looking out, but sitting in the window itself. I painted a real window, too, a long narrow one, with curtains that moved slightly in the breeze. Through the window I put, unrealistically, a wave rearing up, a bit like a Hokusai print.

After a week of working, the only thing that remained to be painted in was the canvas on the easel. What was the artist drawing or painting? I was hurrying a little by then, for I knew that Beth would be home tomorrow. I was due to pick her up in the morning. I wanted to show her a finished piece, but more than that, I wanted to be able to finish the work by myself, alone, the way I had been, luxuriously, all these days. I stepped back and looked at the painting, at myself. And it came to me, with something of a shock, that I had given my eyes that same quality of yearning I remembered from years ago. Surely that yearning had been satisfied by now? I had a good job, tenure. My contribution to a book on Scandinavian women artists, a chapter on Oda Krohg, had recently been published. I was considered an expert in my field. I had a loving relationship with a woman who was herself an artist.

Surely I couldn't want anything more. Surely I wasn't still thinking about Monika Diechmann after all these years, and wishing something more could have happened. What had she given me that Beth couldn't, Beth who had infinitely more to give?

I flipped through the photos again and tried to remember Monika. I read the letters. They seemed so serious now, so abstract. I remembered the great question I had tried to answer ten years ago: What are the conditions for the artistic life of a woman? Now I would have only two words on my list:

Love

Solitude

Finally I looked again at the sketchbooks and the watercolors, and then I began to paint Monika's figure, narrow shouldered, high-breasted, slightly pregnant, on the canvas of the easel my own self turned her hand to. And as I drew I touched the past again, touched Monika, my distant dream of Monika, on every part of her body.

I used to think that the point of falling in love was to make the other person fall in love with you. I used to think that loving had a point, which was to bring you closer to a stranger and break down the barriers of separateness, to make her family. Mostly I still believe that; it's the kind of love my relationship with Beth is based on. But I also know something else, that only Monika taught me. That some people are in our lives to wake us up. We call it love, but it is really something else. We just don't have the words for what they do to us and how they make us feel. We call it love, but it's more like a wave of salt water full in the face. Just for instant it wakes us up, it makes us feel fully alive. And then it's gone; it slips back into the ocean and disappears as if it never had a shape and a word to go with it. Leaving nothing but the taste of salt on our skin and a distant roaring, as of longing, in our ears.

Part Two

We Didn't See It

Gwen was the one everybody liked. She was short and chubby, with ringleted brown hair, round cheeks, and innocent blue eyes, a natural performer. People looked up with a smile when she came into the room; they knew that she'd have some outrageous story, some hilarious joke to share, that her presence would lift and cheer them, make them remember the humor of being a woman, of being a lesbian.

"So I said to him." Pause. "What'd I say, honey? What would *you* have said? No, you're wrong. I didn't tell him to go stuff his balls in a garbage can and give it to the trash compactors..." General laughter. "I said, 'I'm the assistant manager of this warehouse, and if you keep sticking your little prick in my face, I'm going to put it in the paper cutter and get rid of it for good.' " Gasps of hysteria.

"No, you didn't?"

"Hell, no man is going to push me around," she laughed, and punched her right fist into the flat of her open left palm. Her hands were small and fat and ringed with intricate silver and turquoise bands. She waved them around a lot when she talked and was always punching herself playfully, the one hand into the other. It made a fast, threatening crack.

I admired her, but I didn't like her all that much. I guessed I was the only one who didn't.

I said to Miriam after a few visits to her new collective household, "I don't like the way Gwen talks to Amy."

Amy was Gwen's lover. She was tallish, quiet, studious-looking, with a brush of stiff blond hair and small, unobtrusive breasts. She was always wearing a different T-shirt, each one with a slogan about women or a women's event. Amy was friendly but remote, and at first I wasn't sure if she lived in the house or not. She smoked and wasn't allowed to inside, so she was constantly slipping out to the front or back porch in the middle of conversations. Especially when Gwen was telling a story. "Goddamn cancer sticks," Gwen would throw after her, to the general amusement. "Well, don't think I'm going to take care of you when you get emphysema."

"Oh, well," said Miriam, twining her long black hair around her wrist like a bracelet. "Couples, we all know how they get after a while...Amy probably doesn't like Gwen showing off. But she's so funny. I can't believe she talks like that to the guys at work. She's got spunk."

"Yes," I said, and nothing more. Miriam was new in the household and eager to be accepted. I was a recent friend of Miriam's and needed her approval.

Still, a week or so later, after spending the night with her for the first time, I said, "I heard Gwen just now, when I went to the bathroom. She was talking really loud, and her voice went on and on...I couldn't hear Amy." I paused and gazed, suddenly shy, at Miriam over in the bed. It was early morning, and the light from the window settled on her face and shoulders like a soft yellow porcelain glaze. "Well, it just scared me somehow, that's all. The tone of it or something…"

Miriam pulled the covers up and looked at me with sleepy exasperation. Her black hair hung over her shoulders in two ropes, touched with gold.

"Hey, come on, people have a right to their privacy, Diane. How do you know what they were talking about, arguing about? You shouldn't have listened, you wouldn't want anyone to listen to us, would you?"

"We haven't even had our first fight yet." I laughed uneasily and added, "I wasn't *really* listening…" That wasn't true. I had heard the words quite clearly through the bathroom wall: "You goddamned lying cunt." And now they wouldn't leave me alone.

"What if it were a man?" I suddenly asked. "A man talking like that to a woman in this house?"

"Forget it, would you? Come on," Miriam said, and held out a hand to me, smiling. "There are no men here, thank God. Just lesbians."

After that I was often over at the house. I wasn't exactly in love with Miriam, but I thought she was beautiful, with her long black hair and green eyes, her forthrightness and challenging spirit. *Here's a person I could fight with and feel good about it,* I sometimes thought, remembering the sly digs and subtle jabs of Bev, the woman I'd been with for two years. But Miriam and I didn't fight, and I was just as glad. I didn't like fighting all that much.

It was summer, and I was unemployed. Miriam, with a Ph.D. in comparative lit, got up early every morning to make croissants for a French bakery. It was pleasant to lie around in her cool dim bedroom after she left, reading her novels and books of essays, lingering in her scent, Hungary Water, she'd said it was. Later, I would sit on her front porch waiting for her to come home. I had plenty of time to get to know the women in the house: Nelda, the housepainter, Betty, the grad student, Karen, the waitress. I helped them water the lawn and weed the garden; they were always friendly and made me feel at home. Gwen did too.

Amy was the only one I couldn't get a handle on. I knew she worked with deaf children at a special school, and as far as I could tell, that's all she did, aside from smoke and listen and quietly clean up after the others.

"Here my Amy can sign and everything," Gwen said once, pushing Amy forward in the kitchen. "And she won't even think of volunteering to sign in concerts or lectures or anything. I tell her she's letting the women's movement down, and she says she's *shy.*"

"It's the work I do all day," Amy protested mildly. "I want to do something different in the evening."

"If only you did!" Gwen seemed to be teasing; her blue eyes were merry, but her tone was sharp. "You let everyone else do the talking. Shy!" she repeated, throwing up her small fat hands so the turquoise and silver shivered under the light. "If I was like you the world would have run me over a long time ago. But then, I guess I didn't grow up on the Rancho Nuevo Estates, *my* father wasn't a bank vice president..."

"I'm not shy," Amy said, and left the room for a cigarette.

"What do they see in each other? How did they ever get together?" I demanded later that evening. Miriam stood brushing her long hair in front of the mirror, dreamy.

"Opposites attract."

"Thank you, Professor."

Miriam laughed. "I suppose Amy calms Gwen down, lets her talk and act out. Gwen's under so much pressure at work—you've heard her stories, those guys are complete assholes, most of them. And she doesn't get support from the women either. But she won't quit, she won't back down. She's determined to control the situation. Of course it stresses her out." Miriam tugged at a knot, winced.

"So what does Amy get out of it?"

Miriam suddenly looked impatient. She threw down her brush and hopped into bed. "I don't know—excitement, maybe. Gwen's fun and lively to be around. How the hell should I know? You're always so fucking curious about other people. Leave them alone. They're together because they want to be. If they didn't want to be together, they wouldn't be."

"It's that simple, is it?"

"That's why we're together, isn't it?" Her lip curled up, ironic or nasty, I couldn't tell.

My heart pounded strangely, violently, and my skin flushed and froze. "Well, good night then," I said, and turned out the light, getting in next to her.

We lay side by side and I smelled the sweet, nostalgic scent of Hungary Water.

"If you trusted me, would you fight with me?" Her voice floated above us like a balloon.

"I don't like to fight at night," I said. "It scares me."

It was the beginning of August. I'd been lovers with Miriam for a month. It had been exactly that long since I'd heard Gwen's raised voice through the bathroom wall. I hardly paid any attention to Amy now, made little or no attempt to get to know her. When Gwen made a crack about her, I ignored it as the others did, keeping my uneasiness to myself. I had to admit that Gwen could be pretty funny sometimes.

I felt comfortable in the house, though Miriam and I had begun to have difficulties. We'd had our first fight and then some. She thought I should get a job; she said it put too much responsibility on her. "I come home from work tired and want a little time alone. You've been doing nothing all day and want to go have fun."

"I've been working every summer for 15 years," I defended myself. "I get laid off my job and decide to take a vacation. I can afford it, I deserve it. You sound like my mother."

"I feel sorry for your mother, that's all I can say."

"Yeah, well, what am I supposed to do—make croissants or something? I only have a B.A., maybe they wouldn't hire me."

"That's really below the belt, you know, that's really low of you..."

Gwen passed by the half-open door of Miriam's bedroom and poked her ringleted brown head in. "Now, now, girls," she laughed. "So you're finally getting to be a couple. Congratulations. It's nice to see that other people have problems too."

I wanted to say "not like yours" and slam the door, but

Miriam laughed and reached for my hand. I had the odd sensation that she was binding me to silence, that we were binding ourselves in a ceremony under the mocking, sympathetic gaze of Gwen.

"So, what do you think, Gwennie?" Miriam said. "When Nelda moves out, should we let this one here move in?"

It was the first time Miriam had suggested it, and I should have felt pleased. I'd thought for a while that if I had a room in the house we'd both have more space, that then I wouldn't be so dependent. But somehow it didn't feel good to hear Miriam say it now, at this moment and in front of Gwen, especially when Gwen turned to me with her round face all smiles and said, "Yes, I think she'll fit right in."

Nelda left and I moved in later that month, and immediately everything began to go better between Miriam and me. She was offered a part-time teaching job for the fall and I started seriously reading the want ads. I felt more settled than I had since Bev and I had broken up, felt more certain that Miriam was committed to me and that I was to her.

Then late one night, after Miriam had fallen asleep and I was going to the bathroom, I heard a voice coming out of Gwen and Amy's room. It was Gwen's voice, dry, hard, outraged, unstoppable.

And then, unmistakable, the words, "I'd like to kill you, bitch."

And equally as unmistakable, the sound of a fist cracking against flesh.

I didn't think about it. I threw open their door, saying, "No, please."

They were in bed, in pajamas. The table lamp was on; its

small light illumined Amy, eyes closed, arms wrapped around her body. Gwen said, "What the fuck are you doing in our room? Get out of here."

"You can't do this, Gwen."

"You just stay out of this. We're having a fight, and it's none of your business." Her ringlets were askew on her head, and her cheeks were flushed.

"But you hit Amy, you hit her, I heard you." I sounded almost hysterical. "I heard you."

"You're crazy," said Gwen, flatly and furiously. "Get out."

Amy didn't say anything. She suddenly got out of bed and walked past me, heading for the bathroom next door. I didn't dare touch her, stop her, hold her. Her face was as closed as a still life behind glass; then I saw her eyes. Bewildered, ashamed, guilty, they caught mine and confirmed everything.

"You hit her," I said again, my voice shaking. "You can't do that. You hurt her."

"What right have you to come barging into our bedroom in the middle of the night and tell us what to do? Have you got any idea what she said to me? You think she's so quiet and sweet, that's what everyone thinks. You don't know what she puts me through, it's emotional abuse, that's what it is. She was emotionally abusing me."

"You hit her," I said. "You called her a fucking bitch. You said you'd like to kill her."

"You goddamned spy," Gwen hissed, jumping out of the bed and beginning to cry. "You just heard me, you didn't hear her, you don't know what she did. I didn't hit her, you didn't see anything, we were just having a fight." She rushed toward me and I shrank back, but she was past and gone, down the hall, down the stairs and out the door. Her car started in the driveway.

I went to the bathroom door. "Amy," I whispered. "Amy?"

"I'll talk to you in the morning."

"But what if she comes back?"

"She won't come back tonight." Through the door her voice sounded flat and distant. "Just leave me alone now, OK?"

I went back to Miriam's room, but she was deeply asleep. I turned off her lamp and went to my own bedroom. I was frightened but certain. Gwen had hit Amy and confirmed everything I knew was wrong about their relationship. Tomorrow I would talk to Amy, help her escape, move out, get out of the relationship and the house as fast as she could. I knew the others would support me, that they would be as shocked as I was as soon as I told them.

"It was really my fault," said Amy the next morning. We had walked down the street to a café for breakfast, and she seemed willing, if not happy, to talk about it. "I know how sensitive she is about certain things, I just forgot..."

Amy was wearing a Sweet Honey in the Rock T-shirt, and her blond hair was slicked back damply. I felt as if I were seeing her for the first time: her clear, softly transparent skin, her wide, generous mouth, her warm hazel eyes. She would be good with kids, I thought, patient and kind.

"...you know her warehouse job, and how bad it is. People can never find anything around there, they're always asking her. She's so tired of being asked where things are. Well, what happened is, she had given me a roll of film to be developed earlier in the evening, she'd sort of put it down next to me and said something, and I hadn't really been paying attention. So just as we were going to sleep, I said, 'Hey, why didn't you give me that roll of film?' That was such a stupid way to put it, I mean, it was as if I was doing what everyone at work does to her, making her feel crazy about where things are. See, I didn't just say, 'I don't remember—did you give me that roll of film today or not?' I had to say, '*Why* didn't you give me that roll of film today,' like I was accusing her of not giving it to me..."

"But Amy," I broke in. "She called you a fucking bitch, she said she'd like to kill you, she hit you."

Amy flinched slightly and looked down at her empty coffee cup and then over at the waitress. "We go back a long way," she said, as if in apology. "We've been together ten years, I came out with her." Her hazel eyes were pleading. "I did something awful to her once, she can't forget. See, I slept with another woman, I had this affair, I *lied,* and she can't forgive me. She just gets worked up when she remembers. It's really my fault."

"I can't believe you're saying this," I exploded. "No one has the right to call you names and hit you, no matter what you've said or done."

"We went to a counselor once," said Amy, smiling gratefully at the waitress who filled her coffee cup. "I'm still going to her. I don't know—I've been going through kind of a depressed time, I guess. It's nothing to do with Gwen really, I love her, you know. It's just that I've been feeling bad about myself. I don't have any close friends, and I've sort of lost my momentum. I don't even know if I like my job anymore—it's so *silent.* But when I think of changing, I don't know..."

"The reason you're unhappy is because you're in some kind of abusive relationship. You've got to get away from her."

Amy said nothing for a moment, then asked if I minded if she smoked. I asked if I could have one too. I'd given it up two years ago, but sometimes I still wanted one.

We smoked in silence, then she said, "I've thought about it sometimes, leaving...I've thought about it because—because sometimes I'm afraid of her. Nobody else really sees that side of Gwen, they don't know how she can be sometimes...Once, this is kind of funny, but anyway, we were in the car, I was driving and we were on our way to a potluck with some potato salad. And Gwen got mad about something I said and all of a sudden she threw the whole bowl of potato salad in my face. I couldn't see for a minute, I had to turn off the road. I was yelling at her too, she could have killed us. And it was a perfectly good salad, and then we couldn't go to the potluck." Amy laughed a little. "We call it the great potato salad war."

I felt cold all over. "It's not a joke, Amy."

"I know," she said. "I know, I should...But she won't go to a counselor...she doesn't think anything is wrong..."

"Then I'm going to talk to her," I said. "I'm going to tell her I won't stand to hear a woman called names and hit in the house where I live."

"...And so," I finished, trying to stop my fingers from twisting themselves in my lap, my intestines from twisting in my abdomen. "It's just a personal decision I've made, to intervene in this situation, not to accept it..." I stared almost imploringly at Gwen. "I can't accept it."

Her round face was kind, composed, as if she were a therapist listening to a hopelessly unaware client. By design I'd caught her alone in the house as soon as she came home from work and had forced my nervous prepared speech on her in the living room.

She nodded and smiled, but not in her usual jokey fashion. "There are a lot of things you don't understand, Diane," she said patiently, almost absentmindedly, as she pulled a silver and turquoise band off one of her fingers and polished it on her sleeve. "Amy and I have a long history together. We recognize that we have a few problems and we're trying to work them out. When you've been together ten years like we have you have a tendency to push each other's buttons the wrong way. Amy just pushed my button, she can do that really easily—that's part of being a couple."

"But name-calling, violence," I interrupted, still not accusing her directly. I watched the fluid movements of her plump hands, watched how the silver and turquoise emphasized her gestures, finalized them somehow.

"When I called Amy from work today she told me that she was sorry she'd provoked me. I accepted her apology, and I said I was sorry we'd had a fight too. It was enough for me, it should be enough for you."

"You can't just hit people when they make you mad, you can't call them names."

"I want to tell you something, Diane," said Gwen, still in that eerily patient voice. "Amy has some real problems. Serious emotional problems. We were going to a counselor together to try to work things out, and it just became apparent that Amy was in a deep, deep depression and that she really needed some professional help. The counselor said to me, 'Gwen, I see why you two have problems together, Amy has a lot to work out on her own'—so she just started seeing Amy."

Had they told the counselor that Gwen hit Amy? I doubted it. My voice rose squeakily as I reiterated, "It's my personal decision. I'm going to intervene if this happens again. I won't live in a house where this is going on."

"And I'll just tell you to get the fuck out like I did last night," Gwen said firmly and flexed her hands so one of the big turquoise stones stood out like an extra knuckle. "I don't want to hurt your feelings, but I'll have to. What happens between me and Amy is private, just the way what happens between you and Miriam is private."

"It's not right," I said, like a child who keeps repeating the same answer even though the teacher has told her it's wrong. "I won't stand by and let it happen."

Gwen shrugged, weary of the discussion. "And I'll just tell you to get the fuck out."

The front door opened and Amy came in. She looked frightened, hesitant. Her T-shirt read A ROOM OF ONE'S OWN and had a silk-screened photo of the young Virginia Woolf.

"So come in already," said Gwen. "We're just finishing a little talk."

Amy avoided my eyes, went over to the stereo, and started looking through the records.

"Put on Linda Tillery," Gwen said, and her voice was as cheerful as if nothing had happened.

I felt like a record myself, a record that's gotten stuck in the same place, that can only repeat the same refrain over and over until it seems to lose all meaning.

"It doesn't matter if you tell me to get the fuck out. I won't. I'll stand there witnessing it, I'll try to stop it in any way I can, I'll tell other people. I won't ignore it. I won't stand to hear a woman called names and hit. I wouldn't allow it if it was a man doing it to a woman and I won't allow it if it's a woman."

Gwen didn't seem disturbed by Amy's presence; it seemed instead to make her more confident, as if she were certain Amy would support her. "Look, Amy told me she told you the story of what happened. She as much as accused me of lying about that roll of film. That's exactly the thing to push my button, and she knows it too!"

"But you called her names, threatened to kill her. You hit her."

Amy said timidly, "It's really the names that hurt me."

And Gwen erupted. The calm patience that had ringed her anger snapped apart as she jumped up and screamed at Amy, "You lying bitch, you traitor. You told me you explained what happened to her, that it was your fault. You betrayed me, you traitor, you lying fucking bitch traitor."

Amy stood there, frozen, pleading, palms out. "Gwen, listen, I didn't, Gwen, I didn't..."

But Gwen was gone, knocking over the rocking chair in her fury and haste to get out the door and slam it. Amy ran after her, ran out to the sidewalk, down the block after her.

While I sat there, shaking.

Gwen didn't return home that evening. In the middle of the night she came and moved out all her things. Amy stayed. I don't know what was said between them.

Betty was shocked; she said she couldn't believe Gwen had really hit Amy. "Did you see it?" she kept asking me. "You know how Gwen punches her fist into her hand. It could have been that."

"I heard it, I didn't have to see it, I know what a punch sounds like."

Karen had been on a camping trip; after listening to the story on her return, she said, "And we never suspected anything!"

I wondered how true that could be; they had lived with Amy and Gwen for months.

"Didn't you ever listen to them?"

"People's fights are their own business. As long as they do it behind closed doors, who's going to pay attention?"

She looked guilty, then worried. "Does anyone know where Gwen has gone?"

Neither she nor Betty asked much about Amy, how she was feeling, if there was anything they could do for her. They didn't try to talk to her directly about it. They said things about being terribly sorry that it had all turned out like this. They didn't blame me specifically, but they made it clear I hadn't handled the situation very well.

Betty said, "Of course Gwen felt a little crazy when you said you were going to keep intervening. I'm sure she imagined you'd be standing over her all the time, watching her."

Miriam argued with me too, especially when I brought up the fact that we wouldn't stand to hear a man abusing or hitting a woman in our house."

"There you go again. I'm telling you, it's not the same. You can't talk about it in the same way, using the same terminology. Women are more equalized in terms of size and power; it's not the same thing when they fight."

"But they weren't fighting equally. Gwen was battering Amy."

"I didn't see it, I can't say," Miriam said flatly.

"Don't you believe me?"

"I believe that you've had something against Gwen ever since I moved into this house. You've been determined to find her guilty, and now you have. I just wonder why you've needed to make Amy into the victim and why you've identified with her so much."

I was encouraged that Amy didn't move out, that she stayed. For a week or two she became a kind of obsession with me. If I could only make her see what had happened to her, if I could only understand it myself. I went to the library and the bookstore and got books on wife battering, read them, and gave them to her. Amy read them too and gradually began to talk about what had gone on between her and Gwen. It upset me to find she still thought she was wrong to have accused Gwen about the film; somewhere inside she thought she'd deserved to be punished. She didn't deny that Gwen had hit her, but she didn't seem to think it was that important.

"Hitting's the least of it," Amy said at one of our by now daily breakfast discussions at the café down the street. "My dad used to beat me all the time. You just withdraw, you don't feel it. It's the other stuff. You know, sometimes it's seemed amazing to me that I could hold down a job at all, be helpful to people, do some good in the world, when I felt so bad about myself all the time. This last year has been particularly awful. I've just had no self-confidence at all. It used to drive Gwen crazy. She thought I'd had everything in life—grew up in a nice home, went to a good college, lived in Paris for six months."

I accepted one of Amy's cigarettes, seeing her tall and thin with her blond brush of hair, smoking Gauloises in a Parisian café.

"How did you meet her?"

"A women's self-defense class. She was my partner." Amy smiled, aware of the irony. "She wasn't very graceful, but she put her all in it. I thought she was so cute and energetic. I don't know, she seemed so much braver than me. She was calling herself a dyke, was ready to take on the world. She's always been so verbal. I'm not good at expressing myself."

"And that was ten years ago?"

"Yes. We became lovers. I think our first years were happy, more or less. I learned a lot from her. Everybody liked her—suddenly, from being a loner, I had a social circle. We were in the lesbian community. I wasn't an outsider anymore."

"But then you got involved with someone else."

"Yeah." Amy stubbed out her cigarette. "I don't know how it happened; she was just a friend, and then one day we slept together. It was frightening to feel that strongly. I always thought I'd be with Gwen, and then Marcia came along. I wanted to give up everything for her. She made me happy."

"And she felt the same?"

Amy lit up again. "For a while. We kept it a secret, met each other secretly. You see, she had a lover too. And then her lover found out, and she told Gwen. It was a big mess."

"Why didn't you and Marcia go off together?"

Amy shook her head. "She didn't want to, couldn't in the

end. She wanted to stay with her lover. And so I stayed with Gwen. She's never forgiven me."

"How long ago did it happen?"

"Oh, God, it's ages—seven years ago, I guess."

Betty said she'd run into Gwen at a movie and that Gwen had told her side of the story. Betty emphasized "*her* side" with an accusing look.

"If you'd told me the whole story, Diane, about the film and everything, and about Amy's depression, I think I would have understood a little better."

I felt as if I were going crazy. "You mean it's all right to go around punching your lover and threatening to kill her because she didn't notice a roll of film you left?"

"I didn't see it."

"You're accusing me of lying, then?"

"I only think you interpreted it the way you wanted to. You know how Gwen punches her fist into her palm. I'm sure that's all she did."

"But Amy said..."

"Amy is into this victim thing that I just can't identify with."

Karen said, "I think it's pretty presumptuous, your whole idea of intervening, Diane. I mean, are we moral police-women or what? We need to be supportive of each other's weaknesses, not condemning. We get enough of that from the outside world."

I began to cry myself to sleep at night, with Miriam, then increasingly alone in my room, grieving a sisterhood that was as illusory as anything else, doubting myself and all that I'd seen. I was irritable when I talked with Amy. What was wrong with her that she'd let this terrible thing happen to her? Why did any of us put up with less than what we could have?

Miriam suddenly accused me of using this situation to move in on Amy. She said I'd had my eye on her from the beginning. I said, So what if I had, it was none of her business. But I said that only to hurt her.

I dreamed that Amy and I were swimming in a warm sea that had begun to go cold, like bathwater, and that Amy couldn't talk, she could only sign and that I couldn't understand her. I dreamed I asked her over and over, Why, Why, and she just stared and made gestures I couldn't comprehend, palms out, pleading. I dreamed she was drowning me, hanging on to my shoulders, pushing me down into the water that was so cold at the bottom. I dreamed of Miriam's body like an island, dreamed her long black ropes of hair were lifelines I could cling to, that they were a ladder I could climb.

Miriam came to me and said she'd overheard Betty telling Karen that Amy and I were having a relationship and she wanted to know if it was true. She said she was moving out; she said the whole thing had made her sick, she didn't know why things had to be so ugly and sad and hurtful. She said she'd given Betty and Karen her notice—but would I consider giving up Amy?

I said I'd never been involved with Amy, I never would be.

We cried. We held each other for a long time, and we didn't want to fight anymore. We said we wouldn't fight anymore. We started sleeping together again.

One afternoon when I came home there was a little pile of books about battering on my desk and a note:

"Dear Diane,

Thanks for all your help. I've been seeing Gwen again—I was embarrassed to tell you—and we've worked things out. She didn't feel good about moving back into the house, so we've found an apartment together. I think it will be OK, we just needed a cooling-off period. Hope to run into you sometime.

Love, Amy."

She didn't leave an address or a phone number.

And gradually life settled back to normal. It's six months later and winter now. Miriam and I are still together, still fighting. We both have jobs we like, that's not the problem; we both have our own rooms, that's not the problem, either. It's something deeper, something to do with power and dependency, something to do with respect, something that I don't understand. We know how to hurt each other now and seem to want to.

We still live in the same house with Betty and Karen and a new woman that Miriam has slept with once. None of us ever sees Amy or Gwen anymore. I've heard they're planning to move to California. Occasionally someone will tell a joke or a story, maybe about a man they work with or a woman they dislike, and they'll be mocking or indignant or just plain mean, and again I'll see Gwen's ringed fingers and have the impression of someone with her hands full of silver and precious stones, flinging them away in gestures of contempt, as if they weren't valuable at all, as if it hurt to try to hold them.

When that happens I sometimes leave the room. I've taken up smoking again, and it's as good as excuse as any.

Is This Enough for You?

Two women, almost strangers, are walking through a large college campus at night. It is October, but mild; there's a warm, southerly wind, though they are far north. The leaves are dry and abundant; they skitter in the slight breeze; they crackle underfoot.

The women don't know where they are. They have never been here before.

One of the women, Ellen McDougal, is giving a paper tomorrow. It's on lesbian literature in the United States before 1968. She's been writing a book about it, about Gale Wilhelm, Ann Bannon, Dorothy Baker, Jane Rule. Her paper is called "When Desire Had No Name." She comes from a northern California town where she teaches English and women's studies at a small college and where the fog comes in winter and summer to muffle the spaces between the redwoods.

The woman walking with Ellen is Nan Hazlett, a librarian from a large Midwestern city. She was a radical leftist once, now she spends her free time going to meetings for various urban causes. She lives in the inner city and has a stake in its survival. She is in charge of the women's collection at the university library. She's younger than Ellen by about six years, but neither of them is really young. They are middle-aged feminists who have led somewhat complicated lives, who have been actively committed to the lesbian-feminist movement for many years, who have been lucky enough to have increasingly meaningful professional lives, who have had some periods of despair and many of happiness, who have had therapy, who have run away and come back, who have started over. Several times.

They both have lovers at home.

At first they didn't know that about each other. Now they do. They walk, not touching, around and around the enormous campus, filled with commodious brick buildings from the '20s and tall towers from the '60s. There are lamps at intervals along the path, and then the women can see each other quite clearly. At other spots they're almost in darkness—the leaves swirl around them and they have to trust their feet.

Nan has been in a relationship with Marina for two years. Marina is a potter and a day-care worker. She is fat, even-tempered, good with kids, good with her hands. She and Nan thought carefully before they became involved. They were both on the rebound from unhappy affairs; they wanted to move slowly. So they aren't living together and they don't see each other every night. They're happy together and believe that this relationship is one that can last. For this time they have built on the firm foundation of friendship, not desire. They respect each other, they like each other, they love each other. They are honest with each other.

They have made certain promises.

Ellen has been involved with Cora for five years, and they have been in the process of breaking up for the last two. Sometimes it's Ellen who wants to break up, sometimes it's Cora. Both of them, at bottom, know that this relationship is no longer possible for them, that it has no future. But when it comes time to actually pronounce the words that will set them free of each other, the future seems less important than the past. Both Cora and Ellen have an investment in continuing. Back at the beginning when they were in love, they bought a house, furniture, a camper, a washer and drier, a computer, an endless number of things. They both love their house and their garden. They have two cats and an elderly dog. Most people they know consider them a successful couple, both professional women (Cora is a lawyer), both intellectually stimulating, both fun to be with. The friends who know their problems with each other assure them that it's just a stage: "If you started over with somebody else you'd just have to work out some of the same problems."

Nobody wants them to break up.

Nan and Marina have been faithful to each other; Ellen and Cora have not. Cora had a fling with an old lover one vacation; she came close to leaving Ellen, but instead, for various reasons, the affair brought them closer together. The old lover again left Cora, and Cora realized how much Ellen meant to her. Ellen has, for the last year, been sleeping infrequently with a colleague at work. This woman is married and has two children under the age of ten. Even though Ellen knows Cora would be very upset if she found out, Ellen doesn't think it really causes the relationship any harm. Maybe it even helps it.

Nan and Marina have an unwritten contract with each other to be monogamous. It was Nan who first brought up the subject of her previous "weakness;" she felt that her last relationship had been undermined by a series of flirtations and attractions. There was a time when Nan had believed in and had practiced a mild form of promiscuity, but that time is, she has been grateful to realize, over for good. She no longer wants an open relationship and believes herself a more mature person for having decided that. She loves Marina and the calm, secure life they have together. Nan hasn't been attracted to another woman since she met Marina; she thinks of that fact often, with wonder and with joy.

"It's getting late," Ellen says to Nan.

"Yes," says Nan.

They keep walking.

Ellen and Nan began to talk, at first casually and then with more interest, two days ago at lunch. There was a group around around them at first; gradually the group fell away, went on to the next seminar. Ellen and Nan stayed talking for another hour. They talked about books they'd read mostly, the books they'd discovered. Nan has very pronounced tastes: "Oh, that's a terrible novel," she says. "Idiotic." She likes foreign writers best: Yourcenar, Lispector, Marie-Claire Blais. Ellen likes popular fiction, genre writing, and writers who identify as lesbian. "What good does it do to know that Yourcenar was a lesbian if she didn't write or speak about it?"

They laughed, they contradicted each other, but suddenly, in a flurry of warm embarrassment, they felt they had to part. Ellen stood for a moment looking after Nan. A friend passing by saw her, saw Nan's back, said, "Conference crush?"

"Oh, God, no," said Ellen. "Never."

She was opposed to such things, in the first place on principle and in the second place because she was here to exchange ideas. The atmosphere was too hectic for romance at a conference. She knew—she'd been to dozens of them.

Nevertheless Ellen lay awake that night and thought about Nan. She lay there in her narrow college bed listening to her roommate breathe, and from time to time she put her hands on her upper thighs and pressed lightly, as if to feel a body lying on top of her.

Nan's face was becoming beautiful in her mind.

Nan slept soundly. She thought it had been a wonderful first day, and she'd been quite busy.

The next day Nan and Ellen happened to go to the same seminar together. As if it were the most natural thing in the world Nan came over and took the chair next to Ellen, and began to tease her about being in a seminar about French feminist writers.

"I just came to see you," Ellen joked back, then caught her breath, because it was true. *Don't be a fool,* she told herself violently, then softened, because Nan was smiling at her.

"That's why I came too."

Nan didn't think anything of it. She was so secure in her affection for Marina that she didn't even notice that she had begun to flirt with Ellen, had begun to look at her with different, meaning-filled eyes.

Ellen now thought that Nan was one of the most attractive women she'd ever met. She couldn't understand how she'd fallen so far so fast. *You're a fool,* she told herself as the seminar leader droned on about Cixous. But at the same time a delicious heat began to envelop her. It was emanating from Nan's Levi's-clad leg which was exactly two inches away, parallel to Ellen's black denim leg. At the same moment Ellen became conscious of Nan's neck. Not much was visible, and Ellen certainly couldn't turn her head to stare, but somehow, out of the corner of her eye Ellen started to know a little patch of skin showing above Nan's collar. *I would like to kiss this woman's neck,* she thought. She imagined pulling Nan's collar down slightly and running the tip of her tongue lightly along the skin, murmuring, Nan, darling, Nan...

Are you insane? She snapped herself back. *You don't have crushes, you don't get crushes on women you meet at conferences. What the fuck is wrong with you? You're too old for this.*

Nan was feeling a certain tension too, though she interpreted it as high spirits. Mischievously she whispered to Ellen, "Isn't this woman incredibly boring?"

Ellen choked back a laugh, and suddenly a terrible joy overwhelmed her. *Now* she knew who Nan reminded her of. It was Stacy Collins—from sixth grade. They'd passed notes to each other all day, walked each other home at night, and happily reunited every morning. Ellen remembered how she'd wait for Stacy on their corner the last two blocks before the school and how when she first saw Stacy approaching she'd pretend to be elaborately indifferent, but the closer Stacy got the more unbearable it would become to pretend not to look at her, and Ellen could never hold out, she sprinted toward Stacy and Stacy ran toward her and just before they met, they stopped and started laughing, breaking off the feeling that if they hadn't stopped running they could have run right into each other. Though perhaps that's what they wanted, to run *right* into each other, like a double ghost image becoming whole. This sudden, visceral memory heartened Ellen, and she thought, *Nothing can be wrong with this woman, nothing can go wrong with this woman if she reminds me of my childhood.*

Nan's silliness was turning restless. She picked up a pen and began to write notes to Ellen: questions about what writers she liked, and then minireviews. She didn't ask herself why she was unable to pay attention to the discussion or why her foot tapped constantly or why she found herself trying to be amusing just so she could see Ellen's swift, bright smile. She simply wrote faster and faster, almost snatching the pad out of Ellen's hands to read what she'd written and to respond to it. Nan was hungry for ideas, that's why she'd come to the conference. She didn't know why but she and Marina didn't seem to...but this infinitesimally disloyal thought never finished itself in her brain.

The seminar was over, and Nan and Ellen skulked out, a little ashamed of having been "bad students" (one of the presenters had given them a sour look, Nan recalled), and a little exhilarated. Then they were facing each other in the hall.

"Well, good-bye," said Ellen, and quickly walked off.

This time it was Nan who remained standing, staring after Ellen. The first little glimmer of the danger she was in made itself known to her. *But that's impossible,* Nan said to herself in genuine bewilderment: *You can't possibly have a crush when you're truly in love with someone else.*

She spent the rest of the day avoiding Ellen, but it was as if a virus had taken hold and was spreading rapidly through her system. With something like horror Nan recognized each and every one of the symptoms: her heart was beating quickly, much faster than usual; her stomach felt fluttery; her appetite vanished. The more she tried to say to herself, You're imagining things—*your heart is* not *beating more quickly, your stomach is not* fluttering—the stronger and more violent the symptoms became. They were frightening symptoms because she'd had them before, and they had prompted her, had impelled her, to do rash sweet things that had caused a great deal of trouble for her in her life.

Nan evaded Ellen successfully all afternoon, and instead of eating in the cafeteria that evening she went off campus to a pizza parlor with two old friends. Once away from the conference surroundings she began to feel more like herself. Her friends asked her about Marina, and she talked with great pleasure and pride about the life they had together, how happy they'd been, how this was something they both thought would last. The tension she felt began to dissipate, and by the end of the meal she had rationalized her earlier emotions almost completely. Falling in love with people, having crushes and infatuations, was an old pattern. It was finished. She might still have some of those old feelings from time to time; that was all right. The important thing to realize was that she didn't have to act on those impulses. To act was to destroy. Knowing the consequences freed her from the compulsion to act.

Nan was so relieved to have discovered self-control somewhere in her psychological makeup that she felt the urge to call up Marina immediately and say, "I was tempted, but I overcame temptation!" On further reflection she decided this sounded absurd and might even cause Marina some distress. No, she'd tell Marina when she got home, when she was holding Marina in her arms. They'd have a good laugh over it and maybe Marina would say that the same thing happened to her sometimes.

Nan retired early to bed with a book of feminist literary criticism. From time to time an image of Ellen's large gray eyes and her half sweet, half ironic, always quick smile flashed in front of her eyes. Nan let it flash. Repressing Ellen's face only led to butterflies in her stomach, made her feel as if she were doing something wrong. And she wasn't doing anything wrong! She wasn't going to do anything wrong either.

In her own room Ellen sat disconsolately at her small student desk attempting to write a letter to Cora, a letter that would end their relationship once and for all. Crumpled paper lay around her, she had written six pages and it felt as if she hadn't even begun. She wanted to take all the blame on herself, on her own suspect motives for beginning the relationship in the first place, but every sentence seemed to end in recriminations against Cora. "I wanted a sensible person, a kind person, I wanted a person who wouldn't shake me up, a person who I could live with peacefully into old age," she wrote, and mentally finished, *You're smug, you're dull, all your cases are boring, and so are you!*

Oh, God. There must be some way through this. Dimly, dimly Ellen recalled how happy Cora made her at the start of their relationship. It wasn't a grand passion, Ellen told her friends. We're friends first, lovers second. But the sex had been steady and generous and had lasted on past the second, the third, on into the fourth year. They had thought themselves well-suited, not just sexually, but in other ways as well: values, politics, friends.

It was a mystery, then, why Ellen wanted so desperately now to get away from Cora. It couldn't be because of Nan, that was nonsense. Nan was a stranger, they'd hardly talked, Nan lived in the Midwest, how could they possibly work out a living arrangement? Maybe Nan had a lover, yes, she almost certainly had a lover. And that wasn't how Ellen wanted to end things with Cora either, not by going off with another woman. That was insulting, that was criminal, Cora would never forgive her, and it would make everything worse about the house and furniture, the camper, the dog. The only way to do it was to do it decently and honorably, and then in a few months, when Cora had gotten over it, then Ellen and Nan could...

You are absolutely insane, Ellen told herself, and beat her head with her fists. She hadn't seen Nan all day, and Nan hadn't been in the cafeteria that evening, though Ellen's eyes had darted anxiously around all through the dinner she couldn't eat. Obviously, if a woman is attracted to you she doesn't just disappear. Ellen stood up, pushed the curtains aside, and looked out the window on to the campus. There were women walking in small groups and couples across the square outside the dorm. Was Nan out there among them? Should Ellen go out and look for her? Maybe she could find out from someone what room Nan was in, she could go to her room, they wouldn't even speak, Ellen would push her down on the bed, tear open her shirt, and begin kissing her neck, her collarbones, her breasts. And Nan would say…

Ellen found herself sucking on the tender piece of flesh between her thumb and forefinger, exactly as she had the night of her first dance at 14, when Bob Peck had unaccountably walked her home without kissing her, leaving her to lie in bed with a confused, sweet, inexpressible desire. She wasn't supposed to be wanting to be kissed. She was supposed to say no if he asked.

"Aargh!" Ellen said, wrenching her hand from her mouth and beginning her letter all over again.

"Dear Cora,

"I'm sure this will not come as a complete surprise to you…"

Ellen had decided to be absolutely cool and distant when she saw Nan (if she saw Nan, maybe she'd gone home early, that could explain everything) the next morning at breakfast, but instead her face split into a wide, pure smile.

"Hello!" they both said, and started to talk about the conference and what workshops they'd gone to and were going to.

This can't be wrong, thought Ellen. *Not to feel such a…liking…for her.*

I can feel attracted and not do anything, thought Nan stalwartly, and she said, "Well, see you later," and they got up from the table.

"What about," Ellen rushed in, "dinner tonight?"

"Oh," said Nan, staring down at her feet. "I've got kind of a meeting…actually…"

"Oh fine," said Ellen hastily, thinking, *The conference is ending tomorrow, I can hardly wait to get out of here.*

They stood staring at each other, feeling foolish, crazy, naked.

"Well, bye!" Ellen said finally, brightly, and fled.

Later in the day Nan caught up with her. "I was thinking…maybe we could get together after my dinner, just for coffee or a drink…"

"Well," said Ellen, who had spent much of the day not attending workshops or seminars but wandering this strange city's streets, coming to the decision that she wouldn't approach Nan again, that in fact, given the opportunity, she would spurn her. "All right."

It is now 2 a.m. and the two women are still walking around the campus. Every once in a while they get close to their dormitory, but then they shy away and continue this restless pacing. They have only stopped a few times; they're afraid to stop any more.

They should know more about each other than they do; after all, they've been together nearly five hours. They could have exchanged more information, discussed ideas and books—why, for instance, when they love lesbian literature, aren't they talking about that? But conversation, in the known sense of the term, stopped somewhere around 10:30 in the café where they were both leaning forward into the candlelight, and suddenly Nan said, "I have a lover," and Ellen said, "So do I," and Nan said, with more anguish than joy, "I'm very attracted to you," and Ellen, longingly, said, "Yes."

They talked enough to get the basic facts straight. That Ellen had been unfaithful and was willing to be again. That Nan could not, *would* not. What was there to say after that? They left the café and started walking through the campus back to their dormitory. They are still walking because, even though their minds are filled with clichés and their veins with heavy cream, they still believe that somehow they can say something meaningful about this attraction, make it comprehensible, safe, friendly, unthreatening. In each of their minds runs the refrain, *I don't understand why this is happening to me now.* They want to deny the importance of whatever it is, and at the same time revel in it, acknowledge it. Instead they are silent.

The first time they stopped was just after leaving the café, just inside the dark protective boundaries of the forested campus. Ellen stopped first, said nothing, simply held out her arms to Nan. Then for an instant, it was terribly sweet, an enormous relief. They clung together. But nothing was solved, it was worse. Still, Ellen's lips moved of their own volition to Nan's neck. She had been waiting to kiss that neck such a long time. What a delicious smell of soap, what a very very fine gold chain. Ellen curled the chain on her tongue and pulled at it. Vast violent shudders went through Nan's body. "Are you cold?" Ellen whispered.

"No," said Nan. It was desire. And beads of perspiration stood out on her upper lip. Ellen tasted them when they kissed.

They got lost in that kiss. Ellen wanted to say, I've never felt like this. But how could that be? She was 45, she'd had many lovers. At the moment she couldn't remember any of them.

She said, "I want to sleep with you." Of course she had forgotten that she had a roommate.

"I want to too," said Nan, into her hair. Then she stepped back. "But will I?" She began to talk rather wildly about Marina and their promises, and how she couldn't betray her. And then she groaned as she realized she was already betraying Marina, Marina whom she truly loved. How could she be doing this to Marina?

"No, no," she said, but her hands couldn't leave Ellen's face and hair. "I can't, do you understand?"

"No," said Ellen. "Yes, I understand."

"I don't want to hurt you," said Nan desperately. "I realize I've already started. But I can't go on. We must stop..." She stroked Ellen's face. "Is this enough for you?"

"Of course it's not enough," Ellen said. She tried to pull herself together. "At the same time, maybe it is enough. Just to have met you. To know you're alive. I don't know. I don't know."

That's when they began to walk.

Ellen is remembering something her mother used to say to her when she was a child: "I want to eat you up." She would be hugging Ellen when she said it, pressing her closer and closer, while Ellen giggled. But once or twice Ellen got a little afraid, almost as if her mother really could swallow her up whole just from love. When Ellen was older she pushed her mother away. "Oh, Mom, let go!" But once she had said it to Stacy Collins: "I want to eat you up!" She didn't know what she meant by that, but she meant it. She couldn't get enough of Stacy; she wanted to run right into Stacy, become part of Stacy, or have Stacy become part of her. It didn't matter. Stacy had laughed when Ellen said it; she hadn't really understood. The following year Stacy and her family had moved away, and Ellen had never seen her again.

Enough. What could that mean between her and Nan? When they stop walking their bodies flow together like streams meeting to form a river. Their bodies persist, even though their voices say no, in trying to get to know each other, like two dogs their owners are attempting to pry apart.

Would it be enough to kiss Nan for an hour? For two hours? For two days? Would it be enough to lie down naked with her, to caress her, to bring her and be brought to climax? How many caresses, how many climaxes, how many days, weeks, months, years would be enough? Or does she only want to get to know Nan, to be her friend, to look at her and to love her? Does sex have to be involved? How much would be enough? How little would suffice?

Nan knows that she has betrayed Marina, and her despair is so great that it threatens to overwhelm all reason. The more she kisses Ellen the more she wants to kiss Ellen. Desire becomes need, despair begets greater and greater rashness. What does it matter if she kisses Ellen's lips, neck, breasts, thighs? What does it matter if she and Ellen stand behind one of the sighing trees and slip fingers into wet underwear, what does it matter if they go to a motel, if they go away to another country? Or if they do nothing, say good-bye and part? The damage has been done. The first betrayal will lead to others. To Marina it will not matter whether Nan kissed Ellen or not, whether they made love or not.

The impossibility of her situation suddenly causes Nan's knees to buckle. They find a bench, talk quietly, attempt to talk themselves out of this madness. The desire has become a heavy thing; they've gone past the tingle into the ache, past the ache into the dead weight of longing. Ellen's cunt is so hard and burdensome it feels like a black bowling ball pressing in on her intestines. They kiss, and even as Ellen longs for the kissing never to end, her nerves shiver and snap like icy little twigs in a bitter wind. She begins to cry.

Nan is furious with herself. She's hurt this woman, this woman she would want never to hurt. She's hurt so many women in her life, the list is endless, it won't end unless she stops herself.

"Ellen, Ellen," she murmurs. "Darling, please, honey, we've got to go. We've got to say good night."

Ellen nods numbly, stands up obediently. Something is ending that was never begun. Something is dying that shouldn't have been so alive.

They stand close to each other. Absurdly Nan takes Ellen's hand, as if she wants to shake it. They laugh, and for an instant nothing is tragic, everything is funny, spirited, right. Again Ellen has that unexpected, charmed sense of reconnecting with her childhood, with the child she once was.

"Maybe I'll see you next year," says Nan.

"Who knows what will happen?" says Ellen, with some of her former lightness, even flirtatiousness. By next year she will no longer be with Cora, she knows at least that much. And she steps back from Nan, turns and begins to walk away.

"Ellen!" Nan calls after her, frantic. Then she doesn't know what to say. She would like to apologize, but that's absurd. Do you apologize to a woman you've almost fallen in love with for the love? Or for the almost?

"Yes?"

"You understand, don't you? If it weren't for Marina..."

"I know."

They're apart now, and that steadies them, not to smell each other, not to touch each other. They're both moving away.

Then Ellen stops. Turns.

If this were 35 years ago, in her old neighborhood, if this were Stacy not going away but coming to meet her, Ellen wouldn't hesitate. She would run towards her, faster than she'd ever run before, right into Stacy, right into Stacy's blood and muscle and heart, at peace finally with desire and love.

But it's not Stacy. It's Nan, a woman she hardly knows, rapidly becoming a total stranger again, walking away without, more than once or twice, looking back.

I Met a Dog in the Pyrenees

He was an ordinary dog, a brown dog with white streaks, a shepherd head, and a tail that should have curled back on itself but instead flopped waywardly behind. A mutt, in short, a country dog, a dog with fleas and matted hair, not an old dog but with some of an old dog's problems: a slight limp, a few bare spots in the fur. And yet a young dog, too, with an inappropriate friskiness and friendliness.

"I think this dog is following us," I said to Ans, who immediately disagreed.

"No. No, the dog is just walking along with us."

When I first got to know Ans, I thought her way of contradicting everything I said was charmingly Dutch and refreshing. "She's so blunt," I told friends at home. "The Dutch are like that."

"Ans, don't pat the dog. He has fleas, for God's sake. You're just encouraging him!"

"Oh!" she said. "You always see difficulties where no difficulties exist. So a dog follows us for a little ways. Who cares?"

Ans and I always spoke English, for I knew nothing in Dutch

besides "Please," "I'm sorry," and "I love you." We'd met in a café in Amsterdam a year ago last winter, shortly after I'd arrived for a three-week European vacation. I'd just broken up with someone and wanted to change my life. I first saw Ans through the tiny-paned window of the café; she was writing in a notebook and drinking coffee. I was in the street, in the rain, on a bridge over a narrow canal. The café sign said PANEKOEKEN—pancakes. The woman in the window looked out dreamily; she had a square jaw, full cheeks, and blond bangs the color of wildflower honey. She was wearing a thick blue sweater and a scarf tied around her neck in some foreign way, dark blue with a heaven of stars.

Now it was early April, 15 months later, and we were on a brief and compromised holiday in a country that was neither of ours. I'd come over for two weeks at far too great an expense, and Ans had taken time off from her job as a social worker. We'd spent three days in Barcelona and then had taken a local train up into the Pyrenees, to an area called the Cerdanya.

There was snow on the high ranges above us, but the valley where we walked was green and fertile. We'd taken the bus from the small village where we were staying in a family-style hotel to a larger town, and now we were on the way back, with picnic food, walking along a road next to a swollen river, past farmhouses and barns.

"Ans, that dog *is* following us. I'm going to scare him away." I turned and advanced on him with my teeth bared, growling. He lowered his mangy head and rested it on his paws, with his tail in the air, then leaped up and barked.

"He thinks you're playing," Ans laughed. "Oh, leave him alone, he's just a dog."

"I don't like dogs," I said. "They make me feel guilty. Cats are much better. They're independent and indifferent."

"Don't tell me about cats," said Ans with heavy irony. "I know how you feel about cats."

Ans had not liked my cats when she came to visit me in Seattle last Christmas.

"I thought you said you were unattached," she'd said.

"But Bob and Earl have been with me for seven years.

"In Holland we have cats, but cats do not sleep under the covers with human beings."

"They're cold at night, Ans!"

Most lovers see each other's home soon after they meet and decide within a few weeks whether their interests, values, and histories are compatible or not. With us it took longer for romance and reality to collide, months of postcards and letters and phone calls late at night or early in the morning. We had two routine distances between us: A letter took five days or a week; a phone call was a nine-hour time difference. There were other distances as well.

"It's lovely here," said Ans, to make amends. Her blue eyes were soft under her blunt golden bangs. "Just look at the hillsides with the apple trees in blossoms and the snow-capped mountains. Like a postcard!"

The valley was lush in a way you don't connect with Spain, but rather with Switzerland. Every breath was cool and bracing, and yet the sun beat down as hot as if it were summer. I *should* have been happy. If only it weren't for that damned dog.

"Now, see that," said Ans. "He's going off down that road to the farmhouse. That's where he lives. He's not going to follow us."

"That's a relief," I said, and took her hand. We walked along in silence a few moments. I remembered the wonderful two weeks we'd passed last summer in a cottage on one of the Frisian Islands. We'd spent our days walking in the fresh, salt-laden air along the sand, our evenings in wild scheming: I'd give up my job teaching and move to Amsterdam; I'd learn Dutch; we'd live over a canal; Ans would help me find work. No, said Ans, let's settle in the southwest of America, next to the Grand Canyon, we'll become tour guides and have a little log cabin. No, we said, let's both move to the south of France and go to cooking school.

"Oh, well!" Ans said. "Look who's back."

Our friend was being chased down the road away from the farmhouse by a much bigger dog. Ans ran up to them and threatened the big dog. "Leave him alone, bastard!" And then to me, "I guess he didn't live there."

"Ans!" I said. "We don't *want* this dog trailing after us the whole day."

"Well, what am I supposed to do?"

"I'm going to throw a rock at him."

"That I absolutely forbid."

"He's ruining our whole day."

"He's just a dog. Can't you ignore him? Stop making such a big deal. He's bound to go home." She looked at me with determined cheerfulness. "Let's find a nice place by the river and have our picnic."

We turned down a path and made our way to the river. It wasn't deep, but it was wide. The water sparkled and sang over the rocks.

"This gives me an idea," I said. "Let's take off our shoes and cross over to that spit of land in the middle. I bet the dog won't follow us."

We put our shoes in our backpacks and began to wade. The water came up to our knees, then our thighs. The current was swift and freezing. "Hold my hand!" said Ans. We clung to each other and crossed safely.

"Sorry, Dog-breath," I called back. "Now why don't you go home?"

He advanced a short way into the river, then retreated. Instead of turning around, however, he set up a mournful howl.

"This dog is a real nuisance," I said. "Shut up, Mutthead! Go home, *perro malcriado*!"

"He thinks you're calling him," said Ans. "Look, here he comes."

The dog plunged into the river and began swimming. The current carried him downstream, but he managed to land on our spit. He came racing up to where we had just laid out the bread and cheese on a couple of napkins. He shook his wet fur all over us.

"Ugh, get away," said Ans, jumping up. "On the food."

But I had looked at the dog for the first time, right in the eyes, and felt my heart turn over. This was the reason I hated dogs. When you looked at a cat, you might feel love, you might feel fascination, but you could never quite persuade yourself that it shared your feelings. Dogs were different. Dogs needed.

My voice quavered a little. "Sit down, boy, sit down."

He sat and put his head on his paws and looked up at me.

Ans was amazed. "He likes you!"

I gave him a piece of bread, which he wolfed down. "He's starving," I said. I gave him some more.

"That's enough," said Ans uneasily. "What about our picnic? You know if you feed him, we'll never get rid of him."

"I thought you didn't want to get rid of him?"

"That was when I thought he had a home and was just following us for fun. Now I'm not so sure. We might have a responsibility on our hands."

"Too late now," I said.

We lay in the sun for an hour or so, reading, and then noticed it was getting colder. The dog had rested too, but as soon as we got up and put on our socks and shoes again, he was ready.

He followed us to where the spit connected with the other bank of the river, and then across an emerald-green field to the highway that ran through the valley. The hotel where we were staying was in a village on the other side. At the highway a new ethical dilemma presented itself.

"He's chasing the cars!" Ans said. "Stop him!"

"Dog!" I shouted. "Don't do that. Those are trucks, haven't you seen trucks before?"

He was wild with happiness, dashing after cars and trucks doing 50 miles an hour.

"I can't look," said Ans.

"Idiot dog!" I screamed. Brakes screeched, cars swerved, horns blared.

"Let's run across," said Ans. "Maybe he'll follow."

We dashed through a break in the traffic, but the dog stayed on the other side. Now all our attention was focused on getting the dog to follow us.

"Here, boy, come on, here, dog!"

"What are we doing?" said Ans. "If he gets across, he'll keep following us."

"We can't let him get run over."

"I thought you wanted to get rid of him."

"I don't want him to get run over. What a stupid dog, he's the stupidest dog I ever met." The dog was having the time of his life, barking and running alongside the cars, but suddenly he noticed that we weren't with him. Quickly he crossed the road and joined us. I couldn't help bending down and embracing him. "And don't you ever do that again!"

It was sunset when we finally approached the hotel, with the dog right behind us. My calf muscles ached with the uphill climb, and I was exhausted from the altitude. Yet a kind of peacefulness had enveloped the three of us. Ans and I held hands and talked quietly about where we would hike the next day. The dog trotted behind us, sniffing the sides of the path and occasionally lifting a leg. When it came time to say good-bye at the entrance to the hotel, I felt quite sad.

"Well, this is it," I said. "I know you don't understand but we're going in now and we're not coming out. So it's time for you to go back home. *Remember,* be careful crossing the road."

"Bye-bye," said Ans. "We enjoyed your company today."

When the front door was closed, however, I continued to

think about him. We went upstairs and lay down on our single beds pushed together and looked at our sunburns and scratches and rubbed our tired legs.

"I had a dog once," I said. "Her name was Sally, and she was some kind of spaniel. When we were little, we played with her a lot. She lived in a shed next to the garage out back. She had silky black ears and a soft muzzle and the most golden, most eager eyes. She loved us, and she loved to play with my brother and me. But when we got older, we lost interest, and sometimes we wouldn't visit her for days on end. Her fur got matted because we forgot to brush it and because we didn't give her baths often enough. We didn't like to take her on walks anymore. And her little shed stank because we didn't clean it very often. Oh, Ans." I burst out crying. "We neglected her so badly. My father kept saying that if we didn't take better care of her, he was going to take her to the pound, and one day he did. He killed Sally, and we didn't know, and it was our fault."

"Oh, honey," Ans said, holding me. "Please don't cry, it wasn't your fault."

"I can't forgive myself," I said. "But what could we do?"

"This dog is going to be fine," Ans said. "He probably does this every day; he probably knows these mountains like his back hand."

"Paw," I said, and we laughed. Then on our single beds pushed together, we made love. Ans had the sweetest expression when she was loving me; it was as if her blue eyes could see right inside me to everything that was lost and lonely.

We made love until it was time for dinner, then dressed in warmer clothes, for the mountain air was chill at night and the hotel wasn't heated, and prepared to go downstairs.

The dog was lying in the corridor, right outside our room.

"Someone must have let him in," Ans said and laughed.

The dog jumped up and licked my face enthusiastically.

"What an amazing sense of smell dogs have," Ans was still marveling.

"What are we going to do?" I felt panicky. "What are we going to do?"

"Come on, boy," said Ans. "You have to go outside." She began to walk down the corridor to the stairs. But the dog hung back with me. "It's extraordinary," said Ans. "It's as if he's really attached to you. And you were the one who tried to drive him away at first."

I began to walk toward the stairs and the dog followed me. Some people in the entryway smiled at us. "Is that your dog?"

"No," said Ans firmly. She opened the door, but the dog hung back. I had to go out and then rush back inside without looking at him.

"He'll give up," said Ans.

We had chosen this hotel because it was remote and because it catered to Spanish families, not tourists. It was run by an unmarried man in his mid 40s and his mother, who worked in the kitchen. The owner was called "El Jefe" by the waitress who was in charge of our table and who had served us two days' worth of terrible meals.

"I thought Spanish food was supposed to be delicious," Ans said for the third or fourth time, as our second course arrived: a mound of lumpy mashed potatoes with three meat croquettes jammed into them, like artillery guns on a mountainside.

"It is," I whispered. "Maybe it's just that this is a family hotel. Maybe families eat differently than they do in restaurants."

The dining room was filled with prosperous-looking Catalans and their noisy broods of children. We were the only unmarried females and the only foreigners.

"What are we going to do?" Ans said suddenly.

"About the food?"

"About us."

It wasn't that we'd agreed not to talk about it; it was that we so rarely did, it seemed forbidden.

"Are we just going to go on like this forever, meeting in foreign countries?"

I thought of our lovemaking a short while before. "Ans, maybe I should really try to move to Amsterdam."

She shook her head. "You know it wouldn't work, you wouldn't be happy there...Listen," she said. "I need to tell you. There's another woman."

I hadn't told her about Lee, somehow holding on to the belief that to mention Lee's name would make it impossible for me to ever see Ans again.

"You said you'd tell me!"

"Well, I'm telling you now."

"You said Dutch women were boring."

Ans smiled. "Margot's not."

The third course came: piles of thin pork loin without sauce or seasoning.

"I could have written you," said Ans, "but I was afraid you wouldn't want to see me again. And I wanted to see you again."

"To say good-bye?"

"We're going to have to say good-bye sometime. You've said yourself that it's too expensive, for one thing."

"That's because it *is* expensive, for me. I've made three trips to Europe, and you've only made one to America. And I call you more often, too."

"Think of all the money you'll save."

We looked at the pile of pork, and I found myself getting up. "I'm going to the room. Just let me. Please. I'll be all right. I just need to be alone for a minute."

I went out into the entryway and peeked out the main door of the hotel. He'd left and good riddance. But when I came upstairs he was waiting faithfully by our door, stretched out right in front. He bounded up and licked my face.

"Oh, dog," I said, and buried my face in his mangy fur. "Oh, dog, I'm sorry."

After half an hour I came down. Most people had left the dining room; Ans was sitting alone at our table with a cup of coffee.

"The dog's back," I said.

"Did you put him outside again?"

"It's no use. People keep opening the door, and every time they do he comes back in."

Our waitress came over to ask me if I wanted coffee and I told her about the dog. "He's hungry," I said. "Do you have some scraps?"

She nodded and came back with a plate of pork loin. By this time the dog was in the restaurant.

"It's incredible how he knows where you are," Ans said. "He seems really attached to you."

I fed him the scraps of pork. "I don't know what to do."

El Jefe had been told about the dog, and he came out of the kitchen with his mother to look at him. The waitress pointed with admiration to the dog stretched out at my feet.

"See how that dog stays with her," she said.

"What are we going to do?" I asked El Jefe. "This dog has been following us the whole day, and now he sits in front of our room and won't leave."

"He must belong to someone," said El Jefe. "Someone in the town."

"He doesn't," I said.

"He might," said Ans, with her habit of contradiction.

"He's lost," I said. "You can see he doesn't have a home."

El Jefe conferred with his mother. "I'll take him," he said. "Why not have another dog around?"

Ans and I laughed in relief, and the dog barked. A group of people from the lobby came into the dining room, including El Jefe's brother-in-law.

El Jefe said, "It's all right. We just have another dog," and then he went back into the kitchen with his mother.

The dog lay down again at my feet.

The brother-in-law began to question us. Where had we found the dog, how long had the dog followed us, and on what road? Ans and I told our story again, in bad Spanish and with many gestures. The dog slept deeply, filled with pork.

The brother-in-law was frowning more and more sadly, staring at the sleeping dog. "Fernando is too generous. That dog will eat his chickens. That's someone's dog."

Ans was more ready to believe him than I. "Do you really think so?"

"Yes, I think he belongs to someone in the town where you bought your food today. Of course he does."

"But how will he get back?" Ans asked, and she explained the dog's habit of chasing cars.

"I'll drive him," said the brother-in-law. "You two come with me and we'll find the spot where you saw him and then let him out again."

It was so kind of this man to offer that we couldn't say no. After all, we weren't prepared to take the dog.

"But what about El Jefe—Fernando?" I asked.

"It won't work out," said the brother-in-law. "I know him, he's generous. But the dog will eat his chickens."

My stomach was in a knot, but I couldn't see any way out. El Jefe's brother-in-law led us outside, and we all got in the car. The dog hesitated, but I got in first and said, "It's all right, boy, don't worry. We're going home."

It was a starry, foreign night. In the front seat Ans and El Jefe's brother-in-law attempted conversation in broken Spanish and English, while I talked in low tones to the dog next to me. He was sitting upright, staring nervously out the window. I wondered if he'd ever been in a car before. He looked alert and very handsome; I should never have called him a mutt. All he needed was a good bath and some regular brushing.

I said, "I wish I could explain all this to you. It's just that I live too far away. I don't live in Spain; I don't even live in Europe. Ans and I don't live in the same place and never will. We couldn't keep you." I began to cry a little. This is what I hated so much about dogs: the way they looked at you as if they could almost understand, but they didn't understand and there was no way you could ever make them understand.

El Jefe's brother-in-law was a kind man. He drove up and down the streets of the little town and whenever he saw anyone, he stopped the car and asked them if they knew this dog. No one did. We drove out to the road where we had first seen the dog, and the brother-in-law kept asking, "Does he look as if it seems familiar?"

But the dog was lying down with his head in my lap. He seemed so tired and trusting. He had never been in a car; he had probably never had a day like today. Yet he seemed content.

Ans looked back at us, and in the darkness her face was full and soft the way I first remember seeing it in the café. I'd stood watching her through the window, writing, and then she'd glanced up and smiled at me, with loneliness that met my loneliness, but also promised relief from loneliness, that promised connection, companionship, loyalty, and trust, forever and always. It had only taken a minute.

The brother-in-law drove back to the center of the town and stopped in the main square. "It's more likely that he lives here than out in the country," he said. "We'll let him go and he'll find his way back home, back to the people who know him and care for him."

He won't find his way back home, I wanted to shout. *He's lost his home and made a new one with me. Only I don't have a home here, so it doesn't work.*

The brother-in-law had taken out some cookies and was

trying to lure the dog out of the backseat.

"He won't go unless you tell him to go," Ans said very quietly. "Let him go, honey. You can't keep him."

"Go on, boy," I said, and he lifted his ears at my voice. I pushed him out of the backseat and closed the door. The brother-in-law set the cookies down on the pavement and jumped back inside.

"I feel terrible," he said as we drove off.

"I wish this had never happened," said Ans.

I said nothing, but stared out the back window as we roared out of the square. The dog ran after us for a few blocks, but finally he gave up and stood watching me leave him, with that brokenhearted look in his eyes.

Archeology

You may forget
But let me tell you this
Someone in some future time
Will remember us.
—Sappho

The clearing in the woods was overgrown now, Clare said, but to me it seemed like an open meadow. Perhaps that was because it was early spring, and there were no leaves out yet on the vine maple and Oregon grape that had taken over. Only the sketchy lines of twisted twigs and branches were between us and the dark green hemlock and fir that shaped the clearing into a circle. The March day Clare took me to that place in the country—well over ten years ago now—a weak sun shone, and the wind moved restlessly, as if trying to settle itself, in the evergreens. Black crows flew overhead with the swiftly changing clouds. It smelled like rain.

"It looks very different," Clare said, in a wondering, somewhat dissatisfied tone. She walked inconclusively into the center of the clearing and back again, wearing a heavy old anorak and rubber boots. I stayed behind at first, for I was in twill slacks and a blazer over an ironed shirt. My polished low boots had already attracted clumps of mud from the road where we'd parked the car. Clare had picked me up for lunch at the office where we used to work together and where I still did. An hour later I called my boss to say I wasn't feeling well and would be going home.

"There's a lot of it around," said Frances sympathetically. She would not have suspected me of lying. Clare she would have suspected. But that was partly why Clare had to leave.

I had overstayed my lunch hour because I could never say no to Clare. It had been the same when she worked with me at Boeing (we were in the design division and spent our days making graphs and charts for the engineers); I had always fallen in with her plans. Today had been no different. When she had suggested over lunch, "Take the afternoon off. I'm restless with spring. Let's go to the country. There's someplace I want to show you," I had immediately agreed.

"The main house was here," Clare said, pointing to the charred foundations in the clearing. "It burned after I left. Right next to it was the vegetable garden. We grew everything ourselves. The raised beds have flattened, but you can still see them."

She was standing close to me, the way she often did. There was something in her—southern Italian, grandparents from Naples, she said—that did not like physical distance. Always a touch on the shoulder and a stroking of the arm. She came closer to me than anyone except my husband ever had.

"The tree house. The sweat lodge," Clare pointed the structures out among the firs. I hadn't seen them at first. They looked tacked together with salvaged lumber and tar paper: children's constructions, not built for permanence.

"This was my—our—place," she said, leading me around the side of the clearing to a one-room shack next to a tall Douglas fir. There was a glass window and the door opened and closed. Even so, the weather had entered. The place smelled of the forest, not of people.

"It's...cozy," I ventured.

"We didn't have good boundaries in those days," she smiled. It was a face I loved to see smile, a thin face, olive-skinned with straight black glossy eyebrows, black eyes, white teeth, a faint moustache. When she wasn't smiling, she often looked anxious.

She wasn't much older than me—she was 34, I was 32—but she had been a lesbian for an inconceivable amount of time—since college. She'd been in gay lib, started a lesbian rap group, volunteered in a bookstore, organized concerts, lived on lesbian land in a separatist collective.

All during the '70s, while I'd been married.

There was a table still, but no chair. Under the glass window that was no longer weather-tight, was a shelf that looked as if it might have been a washing area. There were a few hooks on the walls and a rod that still held a washcloth.

It had been a red washcloth once. Perhaps it still was (when was the exact moment that something, having lost its purpose, could be said to have also lost its name?). Certainly, however, no one would ever use it again on her face or under her arms, or pull its wet soft dark redness between her legs. The texture peculiar to terry cloth—thread bunched in loops—had given way to something more like stiff, greenish-brown cardboard. It was greenish because of the lichen creeping over it. If I had found this squarish, flat object in the forest outside I might have imagined it to be a chunk of cedar bark covered with moss. Only the fact that it was hanging vertically from a tarnished towel bar alerted me to its former status—though "hanging" doesn't really convey the absolute immovable rigidity of the thing; it looked so stiff that if the bar was removed, the washcloth would keep hanging there in space, an upended flying carpet.

On closer inspection (the touching of a fingertip to its surface), it seemed, however, that the washcloth, far from being indestructible, was held together by mere threads, or perhaps by memories of the soft young skin it had once stroked, and that those threads were weakened to the point of explosion. It had probably never been an extremely fluffy, *thick* washcloth, the kind that are more like soft caresses than cotton; undoubtedly it had come from a more utilitarian department store like Sears or Penney's, or even a more cut-rate source like Woolworth's or Chubby and Tubby's.

It wouldn't take much to start a hole going. It was clear that the edges of the washcloth, especially the bottom edge, were neither even nor intact, but frayed, so that tiny filigrees of thread feathered out minutely, like cilia in the bronchial tubes, barely visible filaments that fluttered with each breath of cold wind. A slight pull to one of the filaments and it would all unravel.

How many winters had that washcloth lived through, including its early useful years when it had scrubbed and soaped, been balled up and fiercely wrung out? How many years it had survived, helplessly absorbing moisture (for that was its dumb nature) through the window that never hung very well and whose frame was now warped and askew?

While I'd been looking at the washcloth, Clare had been wandering the room.

"God, it's depressing, isn't it? I can't believe I lived here for four whole years of my life. That so many of us did."

"What happened to everyone?"

"Came, went, had meetings, fought, left. There were about a dozen of us, maybe six living here at any one time. The ones who were 'in town' were supposed to work and support those who were 'on the land.' The idea was that we'd trade off."

She ran her finger along the dusty windowsill, found a stone, and handed it to me. "We were idealists." The word had a flat, cold sound in the room. "Or just stupid."

The stone she'd given me was small, rectangular with sloped edges, very smooth, pale gray. I rubbed its surface with my thumb and found it had an odd texture. It was absent any hint of the granular, which even the most well-washed of river stones have. I brought it up close to look at better, and caught, very faint, something meadowy. It could hardly even be called a smell: Only a few molecules bumped up into my nose. Not an entire meadow of wildflowers, only one or two. A stalk of lupine, a crushed sprig of love-in-a-mist, a poppy petal.

It was a bar of soap, hardened to stonelike consistency, but still keeping within it a trapped sense of spring.

I wondered who had brought it here and who had used it. Was it a special handmilled French soap, a tiny feminine luxury in a brave new world, or was it something ordinary, like Dove or Zest? Had one of the women used it with the red washcloth, back when the washcloth had been full of rough vigor and the soap was capable of creating a rich bubbly froth?

Had it been Clare?

Clare sat down on the mildewed single mattress rotting on a slapped-together wooden platform, with a ragged Indian spread pulled half across it.

"A single mattress for the two of you?" I asked, standing awkwardly beside her.

"Her name was Sara," said Clare. "She called herself Sara Nightingale for a few years. A nice ring, don't you think? She was a musician—wanted to be one anyway. I think she's working in real estate now. She was completely neurotic," Clare smiled. "Though around here, it was hard to tell what was really crazy or not."

She patted the mattress to indicate I should sit next to her.

I perched gingerly, half expecting rats to crawl out from the stuffing or the platform to collapse. I noticed that the cuffs of my twill pants were wet and streaked with mud. I still held the bar of soap, the fragrant stone, in my hand. I thought of the two of them, Clare and Sara Nightingale, young women living here on lesbian land, in this small house together, making love on the narrow bed. In my imagination they had a woodstove and a pot of tea brewing, and in the distance there were the voices of other women.

I had lived with my parents until I got married, and now I lived alone.

"It's good to spend some time again with you," Clare said, picking up my hand and studying the palm intently, the way she sometimes had at work, in a way that had both thrilled and disconcerted me. "How's the divorce going?"

"It's final soon, thank God." I sagged a little. Roger had veered between making things extremely unpleasant and looking at me with soulful, even doglike eyes. "Tell me just one thing I did wrong," he had often said at first. Now he was calling to make sure I didn't steal or destroy any of our precious possessions before we could settle on who owned, or deserved, what.

"When I first met you last fall, I couldn't *believe* you'd been married for 12 years," said Clare. She put an arm around me and snuggled gently. This too she had sometimes done at work, bending over me as I sat drawing graphs of lines converging and separating again. Frances had warned me about it.

"I've seen this before, Katherine," Frances had said. "Clare behaving…like this. She does it just to irritate me, I think. Just tell her to stop bothering you and she will. I'll speak to her as well."

I had not told Clare to stop.

"Yes, well," I said to Clare. "You know it was a high school thing, me and Roger. I never thought one way or the other about it. First I put him through school, then he put me. We were kids from Everett who wanted to work at Boeing like our parents, but to have better jobs than they had. That's all we ever wanted."

Clare stroked my hair, as if full of sympathy, and then laughed, "Oh, no, I *liked* that you were married. I really felt I could talk to you. You weren't like *them*." She got up abruptly, as if the room had filled with ghosts, and walked a few steps to the windows. With mock drama, she said, "Now you're getting divorced, what am I going to do? What kind of a role model can you be now?"

I lay back on the bed, used to these sudden changes, these quips and ironies of hers. Once, a few months ago, the day Frances finally fired her, Clare had come home with me to the house I then shared with Roger. She'd drunk up almost all of a six-pack we had in the refrigerator and told me her life story: unhappy home with Catholic parents, four other siblings, mother manic-depressive, father patriarchal and punishing. Majored in English, active in the antiwar movement, came out at 20, didn't finish college, and gave all her energy to political work. The Boeing job was her first real job and she'd hated it.

"I took it to save money to go back to school. The only other things I've done were waitressing and office temping. I can't handle authority. I'm not used to it. I can't stand someone having power over me, especially not an idiot like Frances. I liked drawing diagrams, but everything else...It's just as well she fired me."

"What do you want to do?"

"I want to be a therapist. Does that sound strange? I think I *could* help other people. I understand a lot...from my family, and from living in a collective, about the things that...tear you apart."

Later she had reclined on the sofa and had let me give her a massage. I had bent over her a long time, smelling the strong citrus fragrance of her shiny black hair. I had felt her shoulders and her back. I had stroked her legs from the thighs to the toes. Then I had turned her over and had gradually found my way to her full breasts. She'd had her eyes closed and was breathing heavily as I slowly approached her nipples. Then she abruptly sat up, laughed and said, "But Katherine, you're a married woman!"

I'd started divorce proceedings soon after, but when I'd called Clare to tell her, she'd seemed surprised.

"Roger sounded like such a nice guy."

"He's boring. We don't have anything in common."

"But isn't that the good thing about heterosexuals?" she joked. "They don't merge."

"Merge?"

"Lesbospeak, Katherine. Anyway, I hope you'll think about it, before you make a quick decision."

"I *have* thought about it. I just didn't know I could have anything different from what I had."

"I know," she said, almost sadly, before hanging up.

After she left Boeing I didn't see Clare as much. She took out a loan and started back to school. From time to time she'd call me at work and make me laugh. But she'd never suggested getting together again until today.

I rolled on to my stomach on the bed and caught a glimpse of something cardboard wedged between the mattress and the wall.

I fished it up: a dusty record album. The cover was torn at top and bottom around the caramel-brown border, and the photographic image on the front was waterstained, though still visible. It showed a woman with long hair standing on a rock in a desert setting with cactus behind, Joshua trees I thought, and in the very back, a mountain range. It was printed in a duotone of purple and green which gave the landscape and the woman an eerie look, though she seemed happy enough. She had her mouth slightly open, and a row of front top teeth gleamed white. She was wearing a pair of overalls that looked too long; they lapped over her bare feet. It appeared that she was naked under the overalls; at least, she had no shirt.

Her hands were jauntily placed in her pockets, and I could tell she was meant, or meant herself, to look, not posed, but relaxed and at ease. And yet the green and purple tints, water-stained as they were, gave everything a sad look.

The words at the bottom were faded too; I could hardly make them out.

"*The Changer and...the...*"

"The *Changed,*" Clare laughed. "Don't tell me you've never heard of Cris Williamson?"

I shook my head. Before I met Clare I'd never met a lesbian, or if I had, I hadn't known it, a fact that Clare seemed to find both delightful and very strange. She adored telling me stories, stories that she named "bizarre" and "demented," of screaming matches at collective meetings, of trips across country to something called "Michigan," of the strange antics of a group of women living in the woods somewhere near Granite Falls.

It took some weeks before I realized that all of these stories were in the past.

"Don't you...ever...I mean now...I mean, do you have a...girlfriend?" I asked her once at lunch, interrupting a complicated story of rivalries and squabbling.

And Clare had taken my hand over the lunch table and laughed and said in that cryptic way of hers, "Oh, God, no! Isn't it obvious? I'm taking a break from the whole crazy bunch of them."

I never knew when Clare was joking; that was part of the problem.

I took the record out; it was in two pieces, almost as if someone had deliberately broken it in a rage. It was still shiny black but worn with much playing. I stroked the surface of one of the pieces. Like the soap petrified to stone, the record held within it some secret fragrance, some melody that called to me and that I wanted to hear.

"Was she at...Michigan?"

"Of course. And everywhere else. You couldn't go anywhere for a few years without hearing that stupid song." She warbled a few bars, something about a waterfall, and then came back over to the bed.

"This is like archeology, isn't it? These old artifacts from the glorious days of a lesbian separatist commune?" Clare had in her hand a candleholder in the shape of a woman. She was seated. Her wide lap formed a base for the candle, and her arms came together at the hands to make a bowl. It was ceramic, of brown clay with a blue-green glaze. In the bowl were the remnants of a candle. It was still possible to see that it had been rainbow-colored.

Clare held it out to me, and I took it. It fit the palm of my hand in a pleasing way. "For you," she said. "I made it, way back in 1978 or '79, I guess."

She sat back down beside me. I could smell her black hair, which was so much stronger and more alive than the smell of the meadow stone. She had been letting it grow and it came down to her chin, framing her thin face. She had taken off her anorak and was wearing a heavy sweater underneath. I wanted to touch her, to snuggle her as she did me, but didn't dare.

"We wanted to be self-sufficient," she said, all in a rush. "I would be the potter, and Laura would be the carpenter. Sara was the cook, and Tressa was the gardener. We were the main four, and others came and went, an electrician, a welder, and lots and lots of women who couldn't do much of anything. We had a vision—it seems so stupid now—of a thriving community of women networked with other communities across the country and the world. We dreamed of being independent and self-sufficient..."

"But why is that stupid?"

"We wanted to change the world. We thought we could. But we couldn't even decide what to do with someone who wouldn't wash her dishes!"

It was one of Clare's jokes, but it was not a joke.

She lay back on the bed, suddenly exhausted, and I lay back with her. The mildewed mattress creaked. I could see the pattern of the Indian bedspread close up: gray elephants linked trunk to tail in a never-ending procession.

The light was fading, and the wind had come up even more. Overhead and around us the firs moved in agitation.

"You always talk about those days as if they were terrible. But surely—you must have had fun, you must have laughed and danced and listened to...Cris Williamson."

"We laughed and danced and listened to Cris Williamson," Clare repeated, almost mockingly, but also with a kind of longing I had sometimes caught in her voice. "Sometimes I think—I'd had such a strong Catholic upbringing. And I hated my father. And I was rebellious, *loved* the big marches of the

'60s. And being a lesbian was the most rebellious thing I could think of."

"If I were a lesbian," I said tentatively. "I wouldn't do it because I was rebelling against anything. I would do it...because I loved...someone."

"We didn't know anything about love in those days," Clare said.

Without breathing, I placed my hand on her stomach, and she let me. But when I moved it slightly upward, Clare sat bolt upright.

"Don't you understand?" she said desperately. "I'm through with all that!"

"Then why did you bring me here?"

"I brought you here as my friend, someone safe I could talk to. I don't have anyone else I can trust."

She began to cry.

Sorry now and flattered, I sat up too and put an arm around her, murmuring comforting words: "There, there," I said, and "Don't be afraid. You can talk to me. I *am* safe."

Her black eyes looked at me gratefully. Her hair smelled like oranges.

How much I loved her! I understood now that I hadn't asked Roger to leave because he bored me or because of some vague sense that something wasn't right between us, but because of Clare herself. I was in love with Clare and I wanted to be her lover, however long it took.

"No one else I know would understand," she began again. "It's why I don't have any lesbian friends any more. Why I'm afraid to go to the places I used to."

I put the candleholder to the side and held her close. I

couldn't have imagined jaunty Clare sobbing like this. "There, there," I said.

"I'm seeing a man," she burst out. "It's been a year and now he wants to get married, have kids. It goes against everything I worked for and thought I wanted. Married to a man. Becoming a breeder. Turning into a heterosexual. Flipping. Going straight!" She turned her tearstreaked face to me, and cracked, "Officer, I never meant to go wrong!"

Clare could not resist the funny side of things, even in her misery. But I couldn't laugh. "Who is he?"

"You know him. That cute engineer who was around when you first came. Frances had him transferred to another department, the bitch."

"She's not a bitch," I said, drawing the line.

"She *is,*" said Clare. "I'm not a good lesbian-feminist anymore. I can say stuff like that!"

We stared at each other a second, then moved apart.

"There, I've confessed," said Clare in relief. "I've actually told someone."

"That's really why you brought me here?" I said, dully, getting up and going to the window, staring out. The rain had begun, a fierce spring rain.

"No," said Clare, laughing again, trying to cheer me up. "I was rescuing you from Frances! Aren't you bored with all those diagrams of trajectories?"

I laughed too, in a forced way, and said, "It's freezing here. We'd better go."

We closed the door carefully behind us, though there was no reason, and made our way back across the clearing. It had seemed a shorter path than going around through the trees, but once we were inside it, I felt tangled up and persecuted. My good twill pants tore on a blackberry vine, and my blazer was soaked from the rain. Clare strode ahead in her anorak and rubber boots.

During the drive back we were mostly silent. I watched the road, the signs that said GRANITE FALLS, MONROE, SNOHOMISH, EVERETT. She exited there and dropped me in front of my house, the house that was empty and mine alone now, without suggesting that she come in.

Just before we said, "See you soon," I remembered that I'd forgotten the little candleholder in the shape of a woman that Clare had given me.

But like so much else, I didn't mention it.

It's a long time since I went to the site of the lesbian commune with Clare. I run into her sometimes in Seattle, where I now live; occasionally she's with her husband or little boy. He's not so little now, of course; I suppose he must be 11, for Clare got pregnant three months after our excursion, and she married soon after that.

Her husband and I sometimes see each other at work too. I like him well enough. I have wondered if he knows about Clare's history, not that it matters. She probably wouldn't talk with him about it, and if she did, how could he truly understand it?

"I never know what to say to her," complained my partner, Louisa, once after we saw Clare on University Avenue with her son.

It had been a cold fall day, and Clare had on a heavy red

coat that made her olive skin glow. With her dark hair and eyes, she could always carry off dramatic colors. After getting her BA she had gone on to graduate school to earn an MSW and was working as a therapist. I had stayed on at Boeing in the design department and had ended up replacing Frances when she retired.

All our graphs and diagrams were done, easily, on computers now.

Clare and I had a laugh, as always, about the old days at the office, when Clare used to drive Frances crazy, and then Clare said, in that way of hers, touching my arm as if no one but us existed, her face close, her smile so white, that if *I'd* been her boss in the old days, then maybe she wouldn't have quit.

I breathed her citrus hair smell, noticed that she bleached her moustache now. Her face was still a little anxious when she wasn't smiling, but not *as* anxious, I thought.

"She always flirts with you," said Louisa afterward, as we continued down the street to do our shopping.

I didn't try to deny it.

"I never understand these women who suddenly go straight!" brooded Louisa.

We've had this conversation before. "It must have been a hard choice for Clare to make," I'll say, and Louisa will reply, "Heterosexual privilege is not a hard choice to make."

Louisa is my age and works at Boeing too. Before that she was a carpenter in an all-women carpentry collective, but she speaks about it with affection, not disdain. Her longtime lover Paula is still one of Louisa's best friends, and they get together sometimes and tell stories. Louisa has the record *The Changer and The Changed,* and once they played it for me and Paula got tears in her eyes and said, "We had so *little* then. You can't imagine. A few books, a few records, and the things we made ourselves, pottery and jewelry."

"It was so lonely," said Louisa. "To have to create your own reflection in order to see yourself for the first time."

"Singers like Cris Williamson were part of that creation," said Paula. "She made us feel strong and alive and very, very brave."

I listened to the record and heard only a pleasant voice and slightly sappy lyrics. I would never have their early history, much as I wanted to. I had only my own, with Roger, alone and unknowing. He has remarried now and looks puzzled when he sees me, as if I remind him of something he'd almost succeeded in forgetting.

"She probably was never really a lesbian, you know," said Louisa, still rehashing.

"Who knows? Who's to say?"

"Because you can't just wake up one morning and say, Everything I thought I believed is no longer important to me."

"But that's what happened to me with Roger." I laughed and hugged Louisa close. I find it strange, and rather touching, that after all these years together, Louisa is still jealous of Clare.

Louisa laughed too, only partly at herself. "Well, obviously. You went in the *right* direction."

I spend my days with diagrams, so perhaps it's not unusual that I see Clare and my separate trajectories in terms of geometry. Our paths crossed just at the moment I was leaving my husband and she was finding hers.

There was a point in space, an instant in time, when it

seemed we were alike, two women in our early 30s, both in transition, both briefly bisexual, both aware of some possibility between us.

A possibility that was over as soon as the lines of our separate trajectories met and passed.

That point in time exists only in our memories, or perhaps only in my memory. That point in space exists now only in my memory as well. For recently, one Sunday in early spring, I had occasion to drive to Spokane for a weeklong conference. I took the highway that led across the mountains, but before I went too far, I recalled that Clare's commune had been nearby, somewhere in the vicinity of Granite Falls.

The name of the exit was the same, but almost everything else was different. New housing developments keep springing up where there were only orchards and farm or ranch lands before. In search of privacy and the rural life, people keep moving farther and farther out of the cities, bringing suburbia with them.

Where there had once been a clearing and a few structures, there were only bulldozed piles of earth. Another few months and it would have been completely unrecognizable. Happy Valley Glen Estates.

I got out of my car and walked to what might have been a meadow tangled with Oregon grape, vine maple, and blackberry vines, and surrounded with firs and hemlocks that rustled in the March wind. Once there had been a tree house and sweat lodge and a burned-down main house and a little shack where Clare had lived with Sara Nightingale. Once there had been a mattress with a torn elephant-patterned bedspread, and a broken vinyl record in a torn cover and a red washcloth that looked like bark and a sliver of soap that looked like stone. Would these artifacts have been bulldozed into a heap of splintered wood and carted off to the dump?

Or would a few of the small remains have just been plowed under, to be covered up by a grid of asphalt streets and over-large houses with big picture windows?

Somewhere, perhaps, several feet under THE RANDALLS or THE WALLACES, the bar of soap and the washcloth would lie until they completely disintegrated and were no more. The broken vinyl record would exist for decades, perhaps centuries, but it would never be played again, and perhaps no one would know, in times to come, how much those lyrics, so bravely sung by the long-haired woman in the overalls, had once meant to women who wanted and needed to be brave too.

Only the ceramic candleholder in the shape of a woman would keep its name and something of its purpose. In a hundred years or more, when these unbuilt houses too were gone, someone might find it in a vacant lot and hold it up and admire it as ancient.

Would they know that it had been made by a woman who loved another woman? Or would they care?

The spring sky was huge that day I stood in the open field, with piles of earth around me, while below me the remnants of a once-fresh world and its meaning crumbled into nothingness. Except for the figure of a seated woman whose arms made a circle, to hold what remained in memory.

Part Three

Wood

I used to cut wood for her. My parents didn't like it. "Don't go inside that house," they told me always. But they never said why not.

Trudy had been married or was still, nobody knew. The house had belonged to a man named Jim once, then she had come there and he had gone. They had kept to themselves, and Trudy still did. It made her seem unfriendly. It made her seem strange. It made people talk about her. It wasn't just that she was single. There were other widows and divorced women in the neighborhood and no one ever said, Keep away from them.

But I thought Trudy was nice. I was sorry that everybody was so cold to her. She didn't have kids, and hardly anyone ever stopped by to see her. I noticed when cars parked in front and when they didn't. Mostly they didn't. I'm interested in cars. For a while there was an Isuzu Trooper, burgundy, a 1990 model, in Trudy's drive early in the morning three or four times a week. Then it was gone.

I used to wonder if she was lonely. She didn't go out to work but stayed at home. She told me she wrote textbooks, that writing textbooks was something you could do anywhere. It seemed like she enjoyed being at home, working; all the same it was kind of unusual for somebody who wasn't that old. I mean she *was* old, 35 or so, but she wasn't ancient.

My family lived two houses down from her, and didn't have a lot of money, which is why they let me work for Trudy, mowing her lawn in summer, raking leaves in fall, chopping wood down to size for her woodstove. Trudy could have done all that for herself, but she didn't. She said she was a city girl, had never learned. She said she'd be nervous with an ax. I was never nervous.

"It's not really work that a girl should be doing," said my father. But my two brothers were younger and lacked the work ethic. It was good for me to have some extra cash.

My mother said, "Just as long as you don't go inside the house." She sounded firm but also pleading. As if she had some idea of how much I wanted to go inside that house, as if she had some idea of the reason why.

It was my mother who put the idea into my head and kept it there.

Maybe, if Trudy had been more of an outdoors kind of person, I wouldn't have gotten so curious about her. I would have seen her on the road, walking the dog, or getting in and out of her car with groceries, or working in her yard. A lot of women in our neighborhood, which is on the outskirts of town and almost rural, are the active type. My type. The type I always want to be.

So I should have disliked the fact that Trudy was so housebound, even on nice days in the summer. But instead, well, it intrigued me. Because I have another side. I'm not a jock; I don't like sports all that much. I like to read; I'm good in English. I've thought maybe I could do something like writing for a newspaper someday. Or even writing books.

In our house we didn't have all that many books—I usually got them from the library—but I knew that Trudy had bookcases all through her house. Two big ones in the living room. A smaller one in the bedroom. And in the second bedroom, which she had turned into a study, the walls were lined with books, top to bottom. I had seen all these books through the windows of the house. I saw them when I was raking, or mowing, or shoveling snow. How beautiful they looked, some old in faded jackets and others bright new paperbacks with titles that promised worlds. Trudy said that some she needed for her textbook writing and some were purely for pleasure. Most of them, in fact. She said she did more research on-line now, but that nothing could replace the feel of actual books.

I felt the same. She knew I did. She often loaned me books, handing them through the door, saying, "Tell me what you think of this. Each time I brought home a book from Trudy's my mother grabbed it and flipped through the pages. I don't know what she was looking for. She was hardly a reader at all, she never had time for it she said, working all day at Sears and driving an hour there and an hour back every day. But they were only novels, these books that Trudy lent me. Willa Cather was my favorite.

I guess I make it sound like Trudy never left her house, but that's not true. I think she went out during the day, when I was at high school. She went to make copies or to mail packages or to buy more books. Sometimes she went for the whole day to the city two hours away. Sometimes she drove to the city airport and went to another state. She said she had friends there; it was where she used to live.

My parents thought her life was crazy. "I don't know why she wants to keep living here," said my father. "She must feel that she doesn't fit in, that she doesn't belong."

"It would be different if she worked here. *Needed* to be here," said my mother.

"Or if she liked country life..."

"How do you know she doesn't?" I asked them.

"It's peaceful here. It's quiet," said Trudy when I asked her. "I came here because of Jim, and then I stayed. You get used to living outside the city, and it's harder to go back. I get all frazzled when I'm there, see absence everywhere."

She never said what had happened to Jim. I didn't think he was dead, like some people said, people who said they'd seen an ambulance early one morning. Because if he was, he'd be buried in the cemetery nearby, and he wasn't. I had looked.

It was hard at first thinking up reasons why I couldn't go inside Trudy's house. All my excuses sounded lame. Eventually I guess it dawned on her that my parents wouldn't let me. She made a couple of funny remarks about it, but then she stopped. She could see it hurt me. She could see it wasn't my fault. That I would have loved to have come in, if I could have.

So instead, she came out. Not far. Not into the yard much, or as far as the road. She kept close to the house. We talked a lot, if she was in the mood. About books, mostly. The ones she read, the ones she wrote. Sometimes she told me about the places she'd been. Who did she see when she went to the city or another state? She never said. I guessed it was Jim. I imagined that they had had a fight and maybe he had married someone else, and now they were both sorry. I wondered if he had an Isuzu Trooper. I wondered if he had liked to read as much as Trudy and as me.

This went on for about two years, I guess. From the time I was 14, in the ninth grade, till the winter of my junior year. Trudy had been away for quite a while, almost two weeks. The first snows had fallen, and more and more. I had kept her walk clear, waiting for her, and cut up some wood that I'd put by her door. The day she got back I was ready. I'd read that last book that she gave me, *A Thousand Acres,* and I wanted to talk about it. Finally, after school that day, I went by her house and knocked.

When she came to the door she looked really bad. Not sick exactly, but all wasted. Thin, white, tired.

"Did something happen?" I asked.

The cold air rushed between us. I was dressed in a parka and wool pants, with a scarf tight under my chin. She was wearing only a robe and slippers, as if she'd been in bed all day. The robe didn't have buttons; it was velour, like a man's robe, held closed only by a tie around the waist. Something caught at me, below my heart, above my stomach. It was the way the robe opened up over her chest. She had big breasts, swinging free. I'd never noticed that. And a musky sleepy smell.

"Someone died," she said quietly. And paused. "A...good friend of Jim's."

She almost never mentioned Jim. I was pierced. Was she

going back to him, would he come here?

Trudy was shivering in the snowy gusts of wind. “Won't you come in?”

I knew she needed company. I felt so bad. “I want to,” I said. But I could see Mom's truck in our driveway, knew I was visible to her, standing at Trudy's door. “I gotta get home,” I mumbled. “I just came by to see if you needed any wood chopped, now it's so cold and all.”

“I guess I do,” she said, as if she didn't care. “Maybe this weekend?”

“OK!” But just before she closed the door, when I was on my way down the walk, I suddenly called back, “Did you see him? Did you see Jim?”

“Jim?” Her face shattered. “Jim went a long time ago, the first of his friends.”

I stood rooted. The snow was falling thick and hard. Her red robe was a slash of color in the white. “Your husband...died?”

“Jim was my brother,” she said, so low I hardly heard her, just before the door closed.

I didn't tell my mother this news when she asked, “How's Trudy?” in that critical way she often did. As if she expected to hear something bad.

“All right. Going to chop some wood for her this weekend.”

“I thought we might visit your grandma,” Mom said.

“*Mom,* I need the money. Christmas is coming.”

“Oh, all right. I'll take the boys. Dad has to work, but he'll be back for dinner. Can you cook him something?”

“Uh-huh.” If I knew my dad, the moment he heard Mom

would be gone all evening was the moment he'd be joining his friends for a few games of pool. "Don't worry about me, honey," he'd say. "I'll grab a bite at Joe's."

That night, around 9, I took the dog out for a walk. The snow had stopped; it was biting cold, and the sky was full of stars. I felt at home outside; I had never felt lonely, but tonight I did. As if I wanted someone's warmth close up against me, wanted to feel a heart beating through their skin and mine. I took the usual route, but on the way back I went by Trudy's. I was worried about her.

I came up quiet to the house, but before I got close enough to knock, I saw her in the upstairs bedroom. She was weaving back and forth, red-faced, crying. I didn't know if she was drunk or not. Sometimes when my father got drunk he went red and weepy. But Trudy seemed more crazy. As if something in her body hurt her and she was trying to get it out by banging around the room and shouting, "No" and "Why, why?"

I should have been scared. I don't know why I wasn't. I wanted to go in and put my arms around her, get her to lie down on the bed, get her to rest. But I couldn't do that either. The dog started pulling at her leash, wanting to go home. I left the memory of Trudy in her room, shouting. I didn't leave the memory of how she looked, naked.

The next day it was snowing again, and by Saturday the world was heavy and white. I thought Mom might not want to drive, but she was determined. "If the roads are bad, we'll just stay the night."

I waited as long as I could; then I set out for Trudy's. First I shoveled her walk, from the street to the porch, then I shoveled a path around the side to the wood pile. The wood had been delivered to her in logs that were too big for her woodstove, most of them. I usually cut them in half and then in half again. I used the ax from home that Dad kept sharp. I liked the clean way the wood fell in two pieces, then two more. It was a good smell, a sweet smell.

All this time I hadn't seen Trudy. When I was finished chopping, I went to her kitchen door and knocked hard. It took a little while for her to come from upstairs. I was relieved to see that she looked like her old self, wearing jeans and a sweatshirt. Relieved and a little disappointed.

"Can I carry some of this wood inside for you?"

"I thought you weren't supposed to..."

"My parents are gone. Besides, I'm gonna be 17 in three months."

"That old?" she murmured, and opened the door wide.

How wonderful it was to be among the books. I saw that her woodstove wasn't even going. She'd been using electric heat. "You should have told me!" I said.

"The heater is just less trouble."

"But the woodstove looks so nice, with the flames and all. And it's much cheaper, really, heating with wood."

She smiled at me, and that made me remember a lot of things. I asked if I could wash my hands. She told me the bathroom was upstairs. What I really wanted was to see the rooms there, the bookshelves in the study, and the bedroom.

On the way up the staircase, I noticed some photographs that surprised me. I didn't think a woman like Trudy would have pictures of naked men around. The first one was of a black man with his fly unzipped. Then there was a man out in the woods, tied to a tree. And the third photograph was like a crucifixion or saint picture. A man streaming with blood. All these men had erections.

I didn't look around the way I planned upstairs, and when I came down again, I didn't know what to say.

"Is something wrong?"

"I guess...those pictures on the wall."

"Oh, God. I forgot about them. I'm sorry. I know they're pretty shocking. They were my brother's. They're by a famous photographer, I don't suppose you've heard of him, he was gay too."

I stared at her. I knew the word *gay,* knew it from afar. Now it was close. I just stared at Trudy.

"Please don't tell your parents. I mean, for my brother's sake. I mean, for mine. He loved living here, but when he moved here he already had AIDS. Otherwise he probably would have been out. He believed in that. I don't have an excuse. I should believe in it too. I want to be out, but it's so hard. First I was quiet because of Jim, and then when Lin broke up with me, I mean, how could I come out then?" She was talking faster and faster. "Oh, God," she said, seeing my frozen face. "Now I've done it. Now I'll be run out of town for sure."

All these words all jumbled together. AIDS. Out. Someone named Lin, the one who had the Trooper probably. In spite of wanting to tell Trudy it was OK, I wouldn't tell anyone, I found myself walking back out the kitchen toward the door, and out the door.

She didn't try to stop me. She had stopped talking and was

just standing in some kind of horror. I forgot to ask her for my money, and she forgot to give it to me.

Around 5 Dad called to say he was just going to stop off at Joe's for a beer and a game. "Are you all right, honey? Got enough to eat? Heard anything from your mother?" A few minutes before Mom had called to say they'd decided to spend the night. The roads had been bad getting to Grandma's; she didn't want to drive at night. Dad sounded surprisingly cheerful about it. "Oh, she definitely shouldn't drive at night. You're all right, then? Don't wait up for me if it gets late."

I went into the living room and built up the fire until it was roaring hot. Then I stood near it and opened my shirt, as if it were a robe. I touched my breasts, tried to imagine they were bigger than they were, full and ripe and musky-smelling. All those words I had heard this afternoon, I knew them from TV and the news, but now I knew them differently. I knew them from inside. I knew that I had always known them.

When I came outside it was snowing again, really hard. The wind blew swirls of white into the blackness. All the houses on the street were lit up, and their chimneys puffed smoke. Even Trudy's. I came up to the house and looked in the windows. I saw her sitting downstairs by the woodstove reading a book. Except she wasn't reading, just staring out into space. When I knocked, she started.

"I just wanted to tell you," I said before she could say anything. "That it's all right. I'm not going to tell anyone. I don't think it's bad. I'm sorry about Jim. I'm sorry about Lin too." That was the end of my prepared speech, and now I stumbled. "Can I come in, please?"

She didn't move to let me in. Relief was on her face. "I thought, I thought...It's hard to be brave, isn't it? It's hard to be alone."

I wanted to throw myself into her breasts, to hear her heart-beat strong and quick. I wanted to be wood and to burn and burn until I was nothing but heat and light in her hands.

She saw my face. She knew. She said, "We're friends, then?"

I couldn't speak. I nodded.

"It's because we're friends that I can't let you in right now. Someday you'll understand that."

She gave me a light touch on the shoulder and I was outside again. Everything smelled of wood smoke and cold snow.

The Woman Who Married Her Son's Wife

How did it come to this, the three of us with pancake makeup melting in the camera's glare, the talk-show host, Allegra Mostly, demanding that we bare our heart's secrets to the raucous studio audience? The audience is waiting for our story, waiting with curled lips to lunge toward us, to demand, "How could you do such a disgusting thing? How could you betray your son? Your husband?" Will they call me a depraved mother and my daughter-in-law a perverse slut? Will my son be seen as pathetic and ill-used?

I see the audience waiting like lions outside the circle glare of our public trial; I hear them slathering, pretending to be normal, honest Americans who just wanted to attend Allegra Mostly's show because they admire her so much, because they think the issues she brings up are really important.

The only show of Allegra's I have ever watched was on "Men Who Have Sex With Dogs." But that was in the old days, Elise assured me, when Allegra and the other talk hosts were competing so hard against each other. Nowadays they have cleaned up their acts, she read somewhere, pressured by Congress to deal with questions of more substance and decency.

"It will be tasteful," Elise said. "She's giving us a chance to explain our story. Our story could be helpful to other people in the same situation." And Allegra herself was kind enough to call to convince me. "Sometimes love knows no boundaries," she said, in that soft, firm, warm voice that is familiar to millions. "It's important that we talk about that."

It is a hard thing to acknowledge about my lover, now my new partner since her divorce and our ceremony, but Elise, so ordinary in some ways, wants very much to be famous. She has bought a new dress for the occasion. It is short and white, with rather silly puffed sleeves. Her dark cap of hair is shiny and soft, and even before the makeup man got hold of her, she had put on foundation and lipstick and outlined her pretty green eyes with black—she, who always went around in jeans and a torn T-shirt. Beside her I feel ancient and wrinkled in my gray pantsuit and glasses. I am 39. I should know better. The other two are just babies, barely out of their teens.

I remember when Darrell was born and how I rocked him as a baby. I remember his first tooth, his first playground fight, his first girlfriend. He was not a smart boy, nor an athletic one; only good-natured and a little dull. I never understood what Elise saw in him, why she dated him in high school, why she wanted to get married. I told them they should wait; I'd gotten married young, right out of high school. What had it gotten me? A divorce and the financial struggle to raise my son alone. "Wait," I told them. "Get jobs. Go to college." I was speaking more to Elise. "You're growing and changing so much now. In a few years things may look completely different."

Neither of them had jobs at the time of their marriage, two days after high school ended. They moved in with me, into Darrell's room. Elise wanted to get away from her parents. Darrell just wanted what Elise wanted.

It wasn't that I didn't like having them around. Elise and I had always gotten along. We joked and cooked together, watched television, read each other funny parts of the newspapers. She called me her real mother; I said she was the daughter I'd never had. When did it become something more?

Darrell took a job on a fishing boat that summer. He was gone three months and returned in September. He had enough money to move out then, but Elise didn't want to. She said, "Your mom will be lonely." They quarreled and sulked until the following May, when Darrell went out with the fishing fleet again.

The first night he was gone Elise came into my room, just the way she had last summer, but this time it was different. This time she didn't just want to sleep. Sleeping wasn't what I wanted either. Last summer it had been all sweet flirtation and cuddling and delicious tension. All winter it had been awkward and sad. Now everything let loose; we could not pry ourselves away from each other.

"I'm not a lesbian," she said. And I told her I wasn't either. After all, we'd both married men. We pretended at first that we did what we did only because we didn't have men around now. But one day Elise whispered, pressed into the mattress, below my heavy breasts, all my fingers deep inside her, "This is better, this is better than with men."

It was all a secret. We didn't think about what we were really doing, whom we were betraying, until Darrell came home again and Elise said, "I can't sleep with you any more, Darrell. Your mom and I are..."

I remember how he didn't look at me, only went inside his room and closed the door.

"It's not how it sounds," I want to tell the crowd of dressed-up women and men pretending to be decent, normal Americans. "I'm like you. I'm not crazy or perverted. I never knew these things about myself. If I hadn't met Elise, none of this would have ever happened."

She smiles across at me and again my heart stops. That dark cap of hair, those pretty green eyes, that lust for love and publicity.

"What if I had divorced my husband to marry his father? Would you think that so strange?" she is asking the crowd. "It's just the same. Practically just the same."

The audience roars, a hungry lion. My son looks helpless. I, his mother, never prepared him for this. I look at Elise. I feel her bones beneath me. When Allegra asks me why I did it, I can only say, "Sometimes love knows no boundaries."

Suit of Leather

Carter's family, her mother's side of it, had been rich for generations. They didn't call it being rich, nor did they talk about how they had made their money and had kept it. They spoke of wealth. They spoke of managing their fortune well. They spoke of being responsible to future generations. As Carter understood it, wealth was not about money, but about power. Wealth was noticing how people treated you when you said your family's name. It was not about having actual money of your own to spend or having access to the millions that sat, paper-quiet, in banks all over the world.

One of the ways that Carter's family had managed their wealth was to hire a brilliant young lawyer to marry their daughter. Legally, the man who would become Carter's father had no more access to the family's actual money than other sons- and daughters-in-law, for he was not an heir like Carter, only a glorified employee. But he did his job excellently and soon had the family's complete trust. He did not have money of his own, but he had power, and thus he had wealth.

Carter did not remember much about her mother. Slate-blue

eyes, an oval face. In photographs she looked washed out, remote, but Carter had some faint sense memory of orange peels just breaking away from the fruit—her mother's scent?—and she recalled a story about a magical bluebird, the bluebird of happiness, that went together with her mother's eyes.

Her mother had also been named Carter, and she had died—no one had had quite explained how—when Carter was seven, shortly after Carter was sent from San Francisco to her grandparents' home in New York. She did not return to San Francisco except for visits. Her father never remarried, but kept living in the huge house in the exclusive estate and working for the family. Carter hardly knew him. She didn't dislike him, but he frightened her just a little. He was short and quick, rather hairy, and his eyes were clever.

The summer before her 18th birthday she came to San Francisco for a visit. He'd had the cook prepare a special dinner for just the two of them and then had told the cook she could leave early. The maid too. He served Carter himself, explaining about the food, which was light and decorative, and about the wine. At first their conversation was banal, the usual. How was her boarding school and her classes? Carter answered mechanically. He knew her grades better than she did, for they were sent to him regularly; he knew that she would be accepted at Smith, her mother's college, without doing much about it. It would be arranged, as so much had been arranged for her in life.

He asked if she was "seeing" anyone. Of course he knew she wasn't. She didn't mention how she had taken off her clothes once with her friend Sarah's brother on a visit to their house or how afterward, she had let Sarah pretend to be her brother and to do the things Carter would have never permitted him to try.

"Not really," she said.

"Good," said her father. "In your position, you need to be very careful about the motives of people around you."

She nodded and chewed her barely cooked duck with walnuts and pomegranate seeds.

Her father poured them both more wine, and his clever eyes grew brighter and yet deeper too, more secretive. He told her he would like to get to know her better, to start talking with her more regularly about what would happen on her 18th birthday in January, when, technically, she came into her fortune. Of course most of the money was in trust, and she wouldn't be able to touch it, but she would begin to get a regular allowance that was more than she had now.

Carter felt he was looking at her with a kind of hunger and caressing her with his words. He would, he said, continue to manage the family's fortune, which was her fortune, for as long as she found him useful.

"Why didn't you ever get married again?" she suddenly asked him, and for a second he was shaken; then he said smoothly, pouring more wine, "I made a promise to your mother as she lay dying that I would never marry until I could marry someone as beautiful as she was. I've never found that woman."

Bullshit, she wanted to say. *You probably use an escort service or fuck the cook.*

He looked at her sentimentally. "It's uncanny how much

you're growing to look like your mother, Carter. The same blue eyes, the same sweet expression."

That night he came into her room wearing nothing but his boxer shorts. When he woke her up, his erection was sticking slightly out. His voice, oddly enough, sounded as if he were still discussing money. "Just wanted to have a little talk. A man gets lonely. Just wanted to get to know you a little better. You're my daughter and yet not my daughter."

His breath came faster and he tried, clumsily, to unbutton her pajama top. Carter knew suddenly that the reason he wanted her body was not really about sex, but about money and power. She understood that what he wanted to rub his hot flesh against was her fortune, not her cunt. He wanted to possess, through her body, this abstract thing called wealth.

Carter's school, while not progressive, had nevertheless recently sponsored a "self-protection weekend." When she felt her father's hand on her breast she gave a tremendous roar, poked him in the eyes and thrust her knee upwards into his groin. Then, while he screamed, and tried to hobble after her, she ran for the door, and down the stairs to the foyer. In the hall closet she grabbed his trench coat and jammed her feet into a pair of spare galoshes.

She heard him staggering down the stairs after her, trying to explain. She slammed the front door and started running.

She remembered the way to the gate, but in the fog, the streets were lost and eerie. Several times she heard a car slide by slowly. She was determined not to be found, especially since, by this time, she had discovered that the trench coat's pocket contained a wallet with $400 in it and some change. She finally found the gate and the guard drowsing in his little sentry house; she dropped the wallet nearby as she slipped past.

Carter used the change to take a bus into the city and the dollars to buy new clothes. Granted, they were secondhand, but her leather vest, pants, and jacket set her back almost the full sum. Why, when she had no idea where she would stay that night, did Carter spend almost all her money on a suit of leather? It wasn't because as a rich girl she was by nature extravagant about clothes; most of her life she'd worn a school uniform or dresses her grandmother picked out for her. It was only that, walking down the midnight streets of the brightest part of the city she could find, she had begun to see men and women wearing leather: leather jackets mostly, but also vests and skintight pants, sometimes with the buttocks cut out. Heavy leather and smooth as silk leather; black leather and studded leather and leather with painted designs or words. She had never seen so much leather.

It seemed natural, when she passed a shop full of leather clothes (and other leathery things that she did not inspect too closely) to go inside and to ask, "Do you have anything that would fit me?" They giggled at her at first, the two bulky men with their pierced ears and tattooed arms, but they were very kind. They didn't even ask her why she was wearing pajamas underneath her trench coat.

"From sweet 16 to baby butch," one of them marveled when they had encased her in smooth black leather from head to foot. Carter looked at herself in the mirror and for the first time in her life felt completely safe. She was zippered from neck to ankles; they had even found boots in her size and a leather cap that hid her long blond ponytail. She left almost all her money, as well as her trench coat and pajamas, behind when she ventured back out on \to Castro Street, but she felt transformed, both invisible and proudly herself. An hour ago she had been like the girl in *The Nutcracker,* looking at the dance from the outside, still wearing her childish nightclothes. Now she was part of the dance. She was ready to be looked at, knowing that no one could get to her inside her dark, invincible skin.

"What the hell? Hey, wake up, get out of here. Get off our steps, you little junkie."

Carter leaped up. "I'm not a drug addict," she said composedly. "I simply had no other place to sleep."

The woman stared at her and then laughed. She was big and blond, sleepy curls all around her wide face. She was barefoot and in a faded Japanese kimono.

"I get it. You had a fight with your girlfriend and she threw you out."

Carter had been about to confess, "I ran away from home," but she liked this explanation better. "Yeah, that's it," she said, and tried to look both abashed and tough.

"Oh, mama, does it start young. Where'd you learn that look, kid—from old James Dean pictures?"

Carter didn't know who James Dean was. She said, "Around. On the street." She could have added "last night," but thought that simple answers might be best when she didn't really know what she was talking about.

"I guess I should offer you a cup of coffee," the blond woman said, and glanced behind her.

"I don't drink coffee," Carter said. "Actually what I need is a job."

"And you think I've got one?" The woman looked amused again. "Oh, mama."

"Gail? I thought you were getting the paper. Who are you talking to?" A rapid step came down the staircase, and then the most gorgeous woman that Carter had ever seen, tall with silver and black hair, dressed in running clothes, came to stand behind the blond woman at the door.

"Weren't you telling me we needed a new dishwasher at the café, Nat?"

"Yes, for the evening shift. Why?"

Carter didn't register in Nat's dark eyes the way she had in Gail's blue ones, of that she was certain.

"I'm prompt and reliable," Carter said. "A hard worker."

"Where else have you worked?"

"It was in Los Angeles," Carter invented.

"A queer bar?"

"Of course," Carter lied, and then with that little swagger she was trying to develop, "who else would hire someone like me?"

"It would be under the table."

"No prob," Carter said, without having a clue what that meant.

"What's your name?"

"Ricky," Carter said quickly. "Ricky Carter."

"Well, Ricky Ricardo," said Nat, edging past her, "see you tonight. Gail will give you the details." She set off on her run, straight up a hill. What incredible thighs she had. The silver-black hair gleamed in the sun.

Gail was watching her too. "She's my ex," she said. "Break up, don't talk for two years, then start a restaurant and move back in together as friends. Lesbians, eh?"

"Lesbians," Carter agreed.

It was the first time she had said the word aloud, and she relished it.

Nat and Gail's café was open at lunch and dinner and for coffee and desserts in between. Within a week Carter felt that she had been there all her life and that she was part of the small family of cooks and waitresses at Nightingale's. Nat had introduced her as Ricky Ricardo and that was what she was always called, which was fine with her because two days after she started work she had seen, to her horror, an article in the *Chronicle* about a missing heiress called Carter. For a moment, when Carter saw the article and photograph, she forgot that it was her. The newspaper showed a bland, white-faced, light-haired schoolgirl with a forced smile on her lips: her junior picture. She was relieved to see that her father had not suggested that she'd been kidnapped or was in danger; still it was strange to read her name in print, and that of her family, "one of nation's wealthiest."

No one at her new job could possibly connect Ricky Ricardo the leather-clad dishwasher with Carter the heiress, but just to make sure they didn't, Carter resolved never to remove her black second skin if she could help it. She had to take off her jacket off of course; it would have been impossible to work with it on, but she always kept on her cap. They would tease her about it at the café. "Ricky, don't you ever change clothes? Have you worn them so long that they've stuck to your skin?" And once Nat took her aside, seriously, and said, "If you need an advance for some new clothes, some jeans or something, just let me know."

She resisted. The leather was what protected her from anyone seeing who she really was. It was a magic skin over the powerless little rich girl. In her leather pants and vest she strode down the street and looked girls and women straight in the eye. She watched how other women in leather looked at her and how girls in little thin T-shirts that showed their nipple rings watched her. She had never felt tough before she put on the leather; she had been more like the girls in the T-shirts, wistful and avid, allowing Sarah to stick a finger in, then two, then three. Carter knew now that it was she who should stick in the fingers, if it ever came to that. For she was butch. Everybody told her so. Everybody treated her like that.

Her shift was from 5:30 to 11:30. She had all day to walk around the city and to marvel at it. Outside the Castro she lost a little of her ease but made up for it by putting on more swagger. Some people looked at her in distaste, tourists maybe, but there were always women who, even though they were wearing dresses and hanging on the arms of men, shot her glances that were not merely curious.

It was a strange new world. Many of her off hours she spent at A Different Light, poring over books in the shelves and on the tables. There was so much history she needed to know at once. There were so many ideas, so many words, so many stories to absorb. It was like learning a whole new language, a complete anthropology. And Carter needed this rich strange new language not just for herself, but in order to have conversations at work, to invent her past life and to understand what her coworkers were talking about. Because she couldn't ask them straight out, couldn't ask what transgendered meant and how it was different from transsexual, couldn't ask how top and bottom were related or not related to butch-femme or why femme never came first or was sometimes written fem. She couldn't even ask the meanings of the simplest words, words like dildo or diesel or dagger or drama queen. She simply had to nod and laugh or look knowing, and then rush to A Different Light afterward and try to figure things out. The young waitresses at the cafe were either bi or heavily into butch-femme, especially the latter. They flocked around Ricky Ricardo, teasing her with their lipsticks and laces and with the tiny jingle of their pierced nipples, navels, and God knows what else. They would have loved to have worn perfume, but Gail wouldn't allow it: The café had to be fragrance-free, just as it was smoke-free. It wasn't alcohol-free, since marked-up bottles of wine made so much profit, but it definitely wasn't a bar. "Not a bar scene," as Gail said proudly to Carter the first day. "Our emphasis is on food, fresh food, imaginatively prepared."

When Nat and Gail weren't around, the waitresses discussed them endlessly. They all were crazy about Nat and knew details about her daily life. How she ran every day, how she worked out at the gym, how she was totally cool and, like, hardly middle-aged at all. Gail they treated like their mothers. They sighed and rolled their eyes and looked straight through her at the same time as they confessed a grudging respect for how long she'd been politically active. Gail's greatest achievement in their eyes was, however, the number of years she'd been able to hang on to Nat.

"Nat just never *looks* at us," they complained to Carter. "But she's not seeing anyone. We *know*."

"What about Gail, is she seeing anyone?" Carter asked, out of fairness rather than curiosity.

"She's over the hill! She's 40!" they crowed. "Why, are you interested, Ricky? Want to work your way up? Oh, look, she's blushing. Our baby butch is *blushing*."

Carter was blushing because there was someone she was interested in, but it wasn't Gail, even though Gail was so nice to her and Nat didn't even know she existed.

"Where's your family, Ricky?" Gail would try probing. "Do they have any idea where you are?"

"Don't know and don't care."

"But surely your mother..."

"My mother's dead."

"Then your father?"

Carter knew all the vocabulary now. "My father tried to sexually molest me."

"Oh, God, I'm sorry."

"That's why I had to leave home."

"Are you...underage?"

But Carter couldn't tell her the truth about her age. Gail

might have to fire her if she knew. "I told you already, I'm perfectly legal, 19 going on 20."

"When I was 19 I was in college."

"Some people are smarter than others."

"You're very smart! Every time I walk past A Different Light, I see you through the windows, reading their books."

"I buy some," said Carter, stung. "I'd buy more if I had more money."

"But you must want more from life than to be a dishwasher. You could do so much more."

"I'm happy here, just the way I am."

"Oh, mama," Gail sighed.

Other times Gail asked her about her old girlfriend, the one who had thrown her out. To please her, Carter made up a story.

"She was a beautiful woman," she said earnestly. "Lots of curves, blond hair. Around 40, I think. "

"Forty! Wasn't she too old for you?"

"Forty's not old," said Carter primly. "Don't be ageist."

"No, I mean, of course forty's not old....what does she do for a living?"

"Money manager," Carter said, without thinking. "She advised rich families on their money."

"Money manager!" said Gail in disappointment. "I thought I might know her, since she's around the same...since the Castro is a small world. But I don't know any money managers."

"She was more like a consultant or something," Carter backtracked. "She advised people to put their money into the environment and nonpolluting, nonexploitative industries."

Gail looked at her dubiously. "How did you meet? How long were you together? Were you *comfortable,* moving in such high and mighty circles?"

"I didn't move in those circles," Carter said quickly, and then, to shock Gail, "She just kept me around for the sex."

"Oh, mama," said Gail, turning away. She looked as if her knees were about to buckle.

All this time Carter had been staying in a small room behind the café. It had a small toilet but no kitchen. She usually ate her meals at the cafe. Breakfast she skipped. She was trying to save money. She'd never saved money before, had never really thought much about the concept. As the weeks went on Carter gradually began to realize it would take her a very long time to save enough money dishwashing to get an apartment of her own, much less do anything like go to college. She knew that at any point she could go back to the life she'd left, could go back to her boarding school in Connecticut, could go back to a future that included a trust fund and college.

One day she woke up thinking about her grandparents. They were cold and proper people with whom she could hardly have a conversation; still, it pained her that they might think her dead. She made up her mind to call her grandmother at least to reassure her, but when she got through, heard her grandmother say, in that bitter-hard society voice, "Yes, to whom am I speaking?" Carter quietly put down the phone. It was just as well. They might have been able to put a trace on the call. Might have alerted the private detectives, the FBI, whoever else they had working for them. Better not. At least not now.

Carter had left her father's home in August, and now it was November. One night Nat and Gail closed the restaurant down to have a big party at their house to celebrate the second-year anniversary of Nightingale's. All the waitresses had been in a tizzy about it for the last week, huddling together like so many high school girls to discuss what they should wear. Samantha was even getting some new part of her body pierced for the occasion.

"What about you, Ricky?" one of them asked and they all laughed. "Will we see you in something different?"

"I might not be able to make it," Carter said coolly.

Samantha in particular looked dismayed. "But we all wanted to dance with you!"

"Maybe some other time."

It was not that she was tired of her suit of leather, Carter thought as she made her way down Castro Street the morning of the party; after wearing it for almost three months it was soft and flexible and molded her to her body. It smelled like her. She even felt peculiar when it was off, when she took a shower, for instance, and more than one night, when street noises seemed too threatening, she had just slept in it. But all the same, there was a way in which she could see that safe and protected as she was in her suit of leather, she would never get Nat to look at her as long as she wore it.

She took the streetcar down Market and drifted into the Emporium, to the lingerie department. She could at least get some new underwear. An hour later she left, with several packages under her arm. She made another stop, at the drugstore, before she returned home.

The party was going full swing as Carter walked in the door of Gail and Nat's house. She thought she would have to be careful and stay away from the waitresses, but when Stephanie, with a silver chain connecting her lip to her right nipple, passed by her with a casual hi, Carter realized that her new disguise was as effective as her old. Once or twice she saw Gail, splendid in an ivory tunic with strings of beads, glance at her in puzzlement, as if trying to recall where they might have met, but Carter kept well away from her. Even in her silky red camisole and semitransparent harem pants over black lace panties Carter was hardly the most risqué of the younger women there, several of whom were down to their tattoos and jewelry. With her face made-up and her long blond hair washed and swinging free she almost looked wholesome.

At least that's what Nat told her when they bumped into each other in the hallway.

"Mmmm," said Nat, looking at her as if they'd never met before, "you remind me of someone I knew in high school."

"The cheerleader, probably," Carter said. "You were probably on the track team, and you used to kiss behind the football stadium."

"I wish high school had been like that," said Nat, laughing, and by the way she laughed Carter could see that she'd been drinking, not enough to be drunk, but certainly enough to be slightly red in the face and open to whatever might happen. "In actual fact, I was a nerdy science student planning to be a civil engineer. I only dreamed about girls like you."

"Dream no further," said Carter, reaching up to pull Nat's arms around her. "Let's dance."

It was so easy, it was amazing how easy it was. When Carter wore her suit of leather and saw women look at her in the way they did, she was turned on, but not like this. She had to work at her tough look and she had no idea what she would do if they ever responded. But this was simple. She pressed herself close to Nat, and let her fingers trail over her neck and then up her shirt in back, and the whole time she felt amazingly confident that Nat was excited and getting more so.

"I'm afraid to ask, but how old are you?" murmured Nat into her hair. "God, you smell good."

"I'm not going to ask you that question," said Carter. "So don't ask me. Just hold me. Hold me close."

Nat did. Now this was power. Not money power, but wealth of a different kind. The ability to make someone want you. The lights were low in the living room; off in the kitchen, where Gail was, a cluster of women were talking animatedly, but here it was murmuring quiet and sweaty warm. Carter could see a few things going on in the corners of the room that made her feel faint. Stephanie, as far as she could tell, was having sex with three women at once behind the sofa.

Carter had a strange sensation; she was sopping wet between her thighs and she hadn't even been touched. She felt the tips of her nipples tight and hard through the camisole, rubbing against Nat's shirt and hard muscles underneath. The zipper of Nat's jeans caught in the flimsy rayon of the harem pants. Trying to free it, Nat's fingers brushed against her pubis, felt the wetness soaking through the black panties. Her fingers didn't move away, they couldn't seem to.

"I know I am going to make a social faux pas," said Nat in a choked voice, "seeing as we haven't even been introduced, but can I dance you into this bedroom located conveniently behind us?"

"You lead, I'll follow," said Carter. But it wasn't that way at all. How could she have known, based on Sarah's tentative impersonations, so much of what she wanted? How could she have been so ready to arch backwards, muffling her need with one of the coats on the bed over her face. "Give it to me, give it to me," she said. She had read those words in a book at A Different Light, had imagined herself, standing there in her suit of leather, cool and in control, hearing her lover beg for more and giving her everything she wanted. But now Carter's thighs parted wide and she felt herself filling up with practiced fingers until she sobbed and shattered, then floated into a swirl of gauzy particles, a diaphanous shawl or maybe the Milky Way.

"Nat?" someone said. It was Gail's voice, polite and cold. "Are you in there? Our guests are leaving, Natalie, they need their coats."

Nat sprang up. Her black and silver hair was wild, and her pants were down. "Jesus Christ, what am I doing?" she said. She pulled Carter up and pushed her into the bathroom. "Here, I'm sorry, but, God, some of these people are my employees. I don't know what got into me...what's your name? Give me your phone number."

Carter said, "I don't have a phone. Don't try to reach me." She went into the bathroom, which led back into the hallway, and let herself out the kitchen door. She did not feel safe going through the night streets in her fragile clothes. She wanted back her suit of leather. It was only as she fumbled with the door to her small room that she realized she was holding something in her hand. It was a pinkie ring, familiar as Nat's. She must have pulled it off in the midst of everything. She tucked it under her mattress and took off her clothes, got back into the suit of leather, which comforted her with its smoothness and smell of herself. Then she went to sleep.

"Well, you missed a great party," said Stephanie the next day. "I knew Nat had a wild side, but I never imagined that she would actually fuck someone in public at her own house. I thought only sluts like me were into that."

"She...did it in public?"

"Well, practically. She took her into the spare bedroom off the living room, like, where the coats were, and you could hear them going at it like two hogs in heat. 'Give it to me, give it to me,' the girl kept saying. Whew. Hot stuff. I only wish it had been me. But at least we know now what Nat is capable of. Maybe next time."

Carter gulped a little. "Who was the girl? Did anybody know her?"

"Nah. Some straight-looking blond chick with red lipstick and kind of a big butt. Like yours."

"I do not have a big butt!"

"Hey, it's juicy. Come on, Ricky, don't be shy. I had so much sex last night that I'm still horny. How about a little hair of the dog with me in that room of yours off the kitchen? Ten minutes, my butch friend, even five minutes, just suck me off, I'm quick, I promise you."

"That's enough of that kind of talk," said Gail, stomping into the kitchen. "This is a restaurant, not a sex shop. If you want to work at Good Vibrations, Stephanie, I'm sure I could give you a good recommendation." She stomped out again.

"Uh-oh," said Stephanie. "We'll have to keep our heads down today. Gail is going to be in a pissy mood, and I bet Nat won't want to look any of us in the eye."

It was as Stephanie had predicted. The evening was a disaster, with orders mixed up, plates dropped. Gail actually did fire one of the waitresses, the one with blond hair. It was shorter than Carter's, but maybe Gail suspected her anyway.

"It's so incredibly unfair," said the waitresses to each other as they dashed back and forth through the swinging doors. "I mean, Gail and Nat have been broken up for years and years, and now Gail is acting like she *owns* her."

Nat was shamefaced, but also moony, in that strange trance that sex can produce. Carter knew. She was in that trance too, not that Nat was aware of it. While Carter stood at the sink, getting wet at the very sound of Nat's voice, she realized that Nat was talking to her, impatiently. "Can you hurry it up, Ricky? The cooks hardly have a plate to put the food on."

Carter snatched a glance at her. The pinkie ring was gone, and Nat looked dark under the eyes and bruised around the lips. If she couldn't even recognize the woman she'd been passionately making love to when that woman stood two feet away—

well, then, let her suffer. Let her wait and suffer. The time would come.

The weeks passed and things returned to normal. Almost. Sometimes in her room Carter dressed up, secretly, in her red camisole and semitransparent harem pants and lay on her bed and arched backwards, using a dildo she had bought from Good Vibrations (another place of revelations). It wasn't quite the same on her own. She stood in A Different Light reading the erotica books and was confused. What did she want? Who did she want? She loved to walk down the street and see women wilt, she loved it (though was also embarrassed) when Gail looked at her with that silly hungry look in her eyes sometimes and said "Oh, mama." But Carter knew that she could never hope to satisfy Gail or anyone else in just the way that Nat had satisfied her. She didn't understand why, but she knew it was true.

In December Gail said, "One of our cooks is leaving. Want to take a stab at it? You'd be making mostly breads and desserts. I'd teach you."

"Why not just hire a real chef?"

"Because, if you want to know the truth, I don't want you to leave, and I'm afraid you're going to if you don't have any new challenges."

Dear Gail. Carter loved her for her kindness. And she loved Gail even more because she knew that Gail didn't want to sublimate her desire under layers of maternal kindness. She wanted her desire satisfied or at least appeased, just like anybody else. But she was responsible and shy; she would wait for Carter to approach her, hoping that that James Dean look meant something. She would hope until she found out differently.

Because she couldn't give Gail what she needed, Carter started baking, and she turned out to be a good baker. She loved to mix and stir and roll and shape; she loved sweet things and also the slightly bitter tastes of almonds and dark chocolate. Gail and Nat were happy with her, though Gail once expressed some doubt about the black leather. "Are you sure you don't want to wear a nice white baker's smock?"

Carter just looked at her.

"No," sighed Gail. "I guess you wouldn't be who you are without your black leather."

It was Nat's 42nd birthday and Gail was giving her a surprise party, just a quiet one with a few friends and employees after work. Since the anniversary party in the fall, large celebrations had been out, and Christmas and New Year's had gone by quietly. Nat had gradually emerged from the doghouse, though, and she and Gail were on the best of terms again. Neither of them was seeing anyone else. Nat still went around sometimes with a slightly vacant expression on her face, but mostly she looked either sad or resigned. Lately she'd been given to talking about how old she felt. She had pulled a hamstring and it was slow to heal. Then her knee went out. Carter had overheard Gail and Nat talking about menopause and Gail assuring Nat that she was way too young for hot flashes.

To the waitresses, of course, Gail and Nat were practically in an old-age home. Stephanie had resigned herself to the fact that there would be no action with either Nat or Carter and had found herself a car mechanic.

Since Carter had begun cooking and baking Nat had more to do with her, and sometimes when Nat came into the kitchen to discuss the menu she seemed a little bemused when she looked at Carter and more inclined to linger and to chat. Once or twice she asked Carter how long she'd been out on the streets and whether or not she was in contact with her family.

"I'm sure they think I'm dead," said Carter. For she had read another little article in the paper: MISSING HEIRESS PRESUMED DEAD. Her father hadn't waited very long. She wondered if the money would go to him as her closest relative. In a way she wished it would. It would be so much less trouble. But on the other hand, if she had it and could find a way to get at it, she could do a lot of good with it that he never would. She'd set up a walk-in center for girls on the street, for one thing. Maybe build them a shelter.

"Do you have any brothers…or sisters?" Nat asked another time, and then seemed confused.

"Not a single one."

The night of the celebration Carter brought out two cakes. One of them was splendid and three-layered, with raspberry filling and dark chocolate frosting that fit it like a suit of leather. It had 18 candles. The other cake was very small and golden-looking, unfrosted and with just one candle. It had a ring baked inside.

Carter brought out the big cake first, all lit up. Everybody laughed. "Did you run out of candles, Rick? Too many to stick on one cake?"

"Oh, God," said Nat, preparing to blow them out. "I'm so old."

"Actually Nat, that's my cake," Carter said calmly, and in one breath took out all the flames.

There was a surprised silence and then a chorus of "Happy Birthday, Ricky! Why didn't you tell us? We didn't know."

Gail was counting the candles. "Eighteen? Oh, mama, I knew it. I knew you were just a baby."

"Not any more," Carter smiled, handing Nat the plate with her cake on it. It looked small but pretty there, with its golden sheen.

"That looks unusual, Ricky, what is it?" everyone asked, though they were slightly taken aback that Carter had made such a big cake for herself and such a small one for Nat.

"It's a special cake," said Carter. "It's specially for Nat. Don't let anyone else have a bite."

Nat sat and stared at it. "I'm so old," she said, and blew out the single candle. "I'll take it home and have it for breakfast."

Early the next morning Carter heard someone come into the restaurant. She'd been sleeping in her suit of leather, and now she put her leather cap on too. There was a hesitant knock at her door, and she opened it. There stood Nat in her running clothes, looking as wonderful as she had on the first morning Carter saw her. She held out her hand with the pinkie ring on it again. "I had cake for breakfast."

"Was it good?"

"Yes. But what was more interesting was what I found in it.

I lost this ring one evening a couple of months ago. I don't remember some parts of that evening very well, though most people seem to think I made a pretty big fool of myself. But I do remember the woman I was with, and she wasn't you. Do you know her? Can you help me find her?"

"Yes, and yes again," said Carter, pulling off her cap so that her long blond hair fell onto her shoulders. She zipped down her leather jacket, and there was a red silk camisole underneath. Finally she unzipped, very slowly, her leather pants and pulled them down. She was wearing very wet black panties.

"Don't ask me how old I am," Carter said. "Because now you know."

Some hours later the staff began to trickle in through the front door. Carter and Nat could hear them rattling around cheerfully. They could hear Gail, bustling and scolding. Nat began to look worried, but to Carter it was a homey feeling. Especially now that it was coming to an end.

"You know there's no other way out of my room than through the kitchen," Carter said.

"We're never leaving here," said Nat. "We're just going to stay here until you're 30 or I'm dead, whichever comes first."

"Well, I need to get moving," Carter said, getting up and starting to dress. "I've got places to go, things to do."

"Like what, little girl?"

"Like letting my grandparents know where I am. Like opening a bank account so I can receive the first installment of my new allowance. I'd like to start looking for an apartment, and I want to call the university to see about an early admission. I'd be wasting my time back in high school now that I'm ready for college. And, then, if I have time, I might do some shopping. I really need a few more clothes, just for variation."

Carter pulled on her leather pants and vest and jacket. It would be hard not to wear these every day, and she thought that in times of fear or stress or when she needed extra courage and invincibility, she would probably always put them on again. For now she left off the cap and let her hair stream down; how good it would feel to let the wind blow through it again. She put her feet in her boots, and reached over to give the stunned and admiring Nat a kiss. Then, sexually appeased, secure in her love, confident of the future, Carter strode out of her room in her suit of leather to give her friend Gail a great big hug and to ask, very humbly, for her blessing.

Oh, mama.

Silkie

I went down to the sea again this morning, early this morning. I did not see you.

Kelp only, bullwhips of it, and tangled lace, thick upon the shore. Once the people here would have gathered the seaweed into woven baskets, brought it home for drying. Made delicate soup that smelled of the ocean.

Now they eat oatmeal or eggs and bacon with brown bread. There had been a breakfast like that waiting for me. Mrs. Corley had made it for me, as she'd made it every morning for the last six weeks.

She didn't ask me where I'd been when I came in, windblown and smelling of the sea.

She no longer asked me what I'd be doing that day or when I'd be leaving.

I was the last guest to stay on at her bed and breakfast. When I first arrived, in late August, she mentioned that she always closed down October 1 and went to stay with her married daughter in Galway.

It was in autumn that the storms would rush in, nothing between the sea and the hills to stop them, Mrs. Corley told me. The storms knocked out power, the dark came early, the roads were unsafe and the neighbors far between.

"When my husband was alive, I stayed all year then. The farm was going strong then, well, not strong, but going. And it was a pleasure to be in of a winter's night, snug as we were, and to hear the rain against the roof. I didn't mind it. Neighbors would by come by, we had our work to do, and the radio and books. And we told stories then, to pass the time."

I had no stories to tell, but I was always a great reader. I had brought many books with me, as if anticipating a long stay, and when I finished those I took a bus to Galway and carried back another bagful.

"Always reading," said Mrs. Corley. "And what it is you're reading?"

Children's books, I told her. Folktales, too. But mostly books for children.

This morning when I went to the sea it was not raining, but there was a heavy mist. I walked the path from Mrs. Corley's whitewashed farmhouse to a dirt road edged with dry stone walls. There were no other inhabited houses along the road; only a farmhouse here and there with its roof collapsed, its red door splintered off its hinges or faded to pink, or a cottage that was rented out to tourists in the summer and now sat secretive and empty.

About midway between the sea and the farmhouse there was an old school bus pushed off the road, the tires removed but otherwise unvandalized. It was still bright yellow and on the sides was lettered SCOILE (the Irish word for school). In late summer, when I first began to walk this road, the old bus had charmed me. Golden flowering weeds and tall red-hot poker flowers had grown up around it; the windows reflected the sun.

As fall had deepened, the bus had come to have a desolate air, mist all around it like a chill shawl, the weeds tall and gray, scratching at the paint. It always made me remember that this was the first autumn since I'd begun kindergarten that I hadn't gone back to school.

Mrs. Corley never asked me much about myself. Never asked me why I chose to stay on and on in a bed and breakfast in a western corner of the stony Irish coast. From time to time, when there were other guests, I'd said a few things that she must have overheard in the breakfast room, about having been to Europe once some years ago, when I was a college student. Now I was a school librarian, had the summers off.

I lied.

Dublin had been the last stop on a pilgrimage to many of the places I'd gone to years ago, cities where I had hoped and failed to find some remnant of my younger self. I was there a few days, then one morning I'd simply stepped onto a train going west and then a bus, and then I walked until I came to a sign that pointed to a white house with a red door. With a hand-painted wooden sign saying SEAL POINT FARMHOUSE.

Almost everyone else who came to Mrs. Corley's had come by car and because her bed and breakfast was listed in some guidebooks. They stayed overnight, rarely more than three days. They were on two-week holidays and had to see as much as possible.

They came and went and sometimes we exchanged a few words. One morning at breakfast, an older woman, stout, gray-haired and British, rather sharp and inquisitive, grilled me about my work.

"A children's librarian," I told her, aware of how little that conveyed. How could I tell her about the old elementary school on a hill, brick with worn wood floors that echoed late in the day, or about the long room that ran the length of the west side on the second floor, with its many-paned windows and its view of the mountains in the distance. How could I tell her about the books I loved to shelve—*Curious George, Caddie Woodlawn, Matilda*—or about my seasonal displays, autumn leaves, snowflakes, crocuses, resurrected yearly from a cardboard box?

"I'm a children's *author,*" she said and told me her name. I recognized it of course, but pretended I didn't. "I'm here in Ireland to do research," she went on. "I went to Scotland and now here. I've been collecting stories about seals. I thought the people here would be eager to tell stories; that's what I've always heard about the Irish. That hasn't been the case. And I haven't found any actual seals either."

"Maybe it's not the season," I said.

"Perhaps." She told me about her husband and her grandchildren. I realized she was lonely, and unbent a little. Then she asked if I had children.

I hesitated, then said, "Yes. One."

She looked at my finger and did not see a ring.

"Divorced?"

"Yes."

"Then your child must be almost grown-up for you to travel like this." Her eyes, which a minute ago I had seen as lonely and in need of a listener, now struck me as cold and judgmental. I remembered that I had never liked *Badger's Holiday in the Cotswolds* and had thought, *I could do as well myself.*

"No," I said. "She's only eight."

And then I left the room.

This morning when I came to the sea the tide was out. The rocky promontory called Seal Point was almost totally exposed. Once there had been a large colony of gray Atlantic seals who lived on those rocks, but now they were few, hunted almost to extinction, Mrs. Corley had told me.

Only stories about them were left.

I picked my way to the very edge of the sea, over rocks covered with the leathery soft skin of the kelp. The sea was gray-green with a white mist where the waves lapped through the stones.

I stood there for a long time, calling your name. One of the names I had for you.

Silkie.

It already sounded like something lost and long ago. A story I told myself to help myself. A children's story.

I had to repeat it to myself, as I stood there on the empty shore: *No, you were real.*

Bad news comes by threes, I've always heard. This year I learned that for a fact. In my first misfortune I was not alone: All the elementary school librarians in my district lost their jobs at once. The taxpayers spoke and the budgetary ax came down. Children's librarians were a luxury and must go. The mountains in the distant view would remain, but I would not be there to see them. Teachers, my friends already so underpaid and overworked, would help the children choose books and check them in and out. My autumn leaves and snowflakes would stay in their box. No longer would I try to teach the Dewey Decimal system or read a book aloud to a lively group of second graders.

I got the news on a spring day and came home in a rage. An hour later I could barely remember that rage, so quickly was it blanketed by something larger—as if a fire truck had arrived to deal with a sudden hot blaze in one room of the house, and had then hosed water and flame retardant over everything. Destroying it all.

"I know there will never be a good time to tell you," blurted Diana. "But I have to go."

Maybe she thought that, thrown off course by news of my dismissal, I wouldn't have the courage or the anger to fight back.

She was right.

My eyes blinked back shocked tears. I whispered, "Tracy?"

"I'll take her with me, of course," Diana said harshly, for she couldn't afford to be tender. "After all, I'm her mother."

Three pieces of news, all unexpected, and all bad.

Instead of anger, hopeless bitterness in a gray cloud fell over me like ashes.

You came to comfort me, though I didn't know it at first. I felt only what I thought was lust, the desire to be touched again and to touch.

It was about 7 a.m. when I found you sleeping on the shore. No one else was about. I'd woken at four, full of unhappiness. Dreaming of Diana. In that pathetic way of dreams, I'd found myself on my knees, begging her to return, sobbing that there must be something left: We had been together six years. I had helped her raise her daughter, given money, given time, given all the love I'd known how to give.

Waking, my mouth was dry and salty, as if I'd fallen asleep chewing a cracker. I felt self-revulsion to my fingertips. I had never begged, thank God. I had stood aside, in deadened condemnation, while she made moves to leave. In the end, because I couldn't bear to see Tracy uprooted, I left the house we'd bought together three years before and moved in with a friend. A few weeks later, when school ended, I'd emptied my bank account and set off for Europe.

As soon as it was light I came to the stony beach, to burn away the humiliation of feeling anything for Diana still. I came to scour out the longing for the daughter I had once believed, had been told, was equally mine. Underneath my sweater and jeans, I had on my swimsuit, for I meant to swim, as I had been swimming the last week, before breakfast, in water so cold it took my breath away and stopped me from thinking.

I assumed you were French when I saw you lying there, naked, without even a towel beneath you. Mrs. Corley had mentioned that a group of French tourists had rented a house along the coastal road. Your short hair was dark and your pubic triangle black as wet kelp. You were darkly tanned, without any sun lines, and lightly oiled, so that your skin had almost a sheen of water. Your breasts were high and small, your hips wide.

Your feet were thin and very long, your hands the same.

The tide was out, and you lay lightly, as if tossed ashore on the smooth gray stones of the little beach between the rocks. To the side was your knapsack, made of a curious material, gray-black oilcloth perhaps, with a clasp that seemed to be of bone or polished white coral.

I couldn't help myself; I sat on your knapsack, stared at you in longing, willed you to wake up, and yet feared it. For I knew that once you did, you would look at me in horror, would feel, quite rightly, that you had been violated by my gaze. I wouldn't be able to explain in time that I was only lonely, that my lover had turned away from me and left me doubting myself and loathing her. I wouldn't have time to explain, for you would jump up and shout at me in French, something vile about "*perversité*."

You didn't wake up. You kept on sleeping. Gently, like a baby. And gradually I quieted in myself, watching you. As if I were watching Tracy sleep, as I had watched her since she'd been a toddler.

"Could I have asked for anything more?" Diana had once said, a year into our relationship, lying in my arms at night. "A woman who loves my daughter as much as I do."

"Our daughter," I dared to say for the first time, and Diana drew in her breath and her beautiful dark eyes looked deeply into mine and she repeated quietly, "Our daughter."

It was two or three years later that Diana began to draw away from me, by imperceptible degrees. Did she draw away, or did something opaque and heavy begin to form, like condensation on a glass, each drop composed of some invisible wrong step I took? I never knew, and she would never tell me. "You're not doing anything," she would say, impatient. "I'm restless in myself, I don't know why."

All this I thought about and remembered as I looked at you and then at the ocean's horizon. Thousands of miles away Tracy was starting school and Diana was probably with someone else, someone Diana could feel passionate about for a year or two, someone who might also begin to believe that Tracy was her daughter.

When you finally spoke, your voice was strange, with a rough, fogged sound, as if you were getting over a cold. It could have been French or some other older language, like Basque perhaps, or Gaelic.

"Hello," you said. You didn't seem alarmed to find me there, but your large brown eyes were fixed on the knapsack.

"I'm so sorry, I'm sitting on your things," I said, jumping up.

But you never engaged in social chat. With you there were no introductions, apologies, or how-are-you exchanges.

"Take off your clothes," you whispered.

And I did.

If I were writing a lesbian erotic novel, of the sort that had increasingly piled up by Diana's side of the bed, what happened next would be easy to explain. I met a strange foreign woman on the beach. Her nipples were hard, her cunt was wet, our passion flowered and burst before we had time to say our names.

It wasn't like that.

"Lie down beside me," you whispered.

And I did.

Your skin was soft and slippery and warm.

"Don't be afraid."

I wasn't. My eyes closed almost automatically, as if I had been very tired, so very tired, and needed to rest. All the same, my body was awake, and all my senses. I felt the stones beneath me. I felt your skin down the length of my body. I smelled the sharp dank smell of the sea, and I heard the waves rising up along the shore, heard them crash and pull at the stones as the water sucked back.

Heard the tide come in. It touched my toes, very cold, and then my ankles. Moved up.

"Don't be afraid," you whispered again.

And I wasn't. I remembered sleepily how my mother used to dip me toe by toe into the backyard wading pool, and how I taught myself to enter the ocean as a child: foot, calf, knee, and thigh, and all at once, I was in.

Like now, with you.

"Hold on," you said, and I held on, for your arms were moving in the water, powerful arms, and your legs were melded together all of a piece, able to propel us fast and fanlike.

Now you spoke to me no longer. I remember thinking clearly: I must not open my mouth.

I knew it was water we were in, deep water, and that it was dangerous to me, but safe to you.

As long as I held you, I would be all right.

I don't remember much else. No kingdoms of the deep, no sunken palaces or mermaids and sea horses. Only veils of green and dark blue flying past, thin as wet tissue paper, and streamers of golden light flickering from a light source high above.

No sense of cold or of strangeness. More the sense of being

enveloped, held close up to you but also in my own skin.

Rocked.

Then we were on the shore again.

Had we made love?

I didn't know. You were breathing hard and glistening all over with a beaded sweat. My body was euphoric, dazzled in the sudden sunlight, wet.

I fell into a deep calm sleep and when I woke was rested as I had not been in months. My watch said 10; my clothes were neatly piled next to me on the rock where I lay.

Your knapsack was gone and so were you. In the distance, on the rocky promontory, I thought I saw a rounded shape.

From far away you called to me in a long and sweet lament.

I had run out of all my travelers' checks by the time I'd arrived in Dublin, and I'd taken out a cash advance on my Visa card. It was a large enough sum to let me travel in Ireland for two weeks and to get me back to London for my flight home in September; large enough too that I wondered how I would pay it off.

I wrote Diana to tell her I was not returning in September or anytime soon and to ask her to forward my mail to Mrs. Corley's at Seal Point. I enclosed a note to Tracy to say I thought of her often and would have a lot to tell her about my travels when I saw her.

A week later I came in one day to find a manila envelope with my old house as the return address. Inside was the dreaded Visa bill with a Post-It note from Diana: "Call me when you get a chance. Glad traveling suits you."

And a letter with drawings from Tracy that told me all about school and her friends and ended, "I miss you so *much.* Please write soon!"

Mrs. Corley found me crying in the small parlor.

"There, there, dear," she said. "I've got the kettle on. I'll bring you a cup of tea. Not bad news, I hope."

"No, no," I said (though the Visa bill was definitely a problem). "It's from a little girl I know."

"Your daughter?" she asked, and it was the most personal question she'd ever ventured. It shot past her usual reserve.

"Yes. I mean. She was…it's hard to explain."

"But you miss her."

"Yes."

Just to say it aloud was a relief. Mrs. Corley came back with a pot and two cups. She didn't ask more questions, but began to talk on quite another subject.

"Have you heard the seal out on the rocks? I heard it last week a time or two and then again today. It's just the one seal. There used to be so many. Hunted off a long while ago. Just the one now and making quite a noise sometimes. There's some say that a seal sounds like a baby crying or a woman. They've a kind of human sound to them. Asking for something."

"For what?" I drank my tea and didn't meet her eyes.

"To be a relation to us maybe. You know a seal is an animal that can't be at ease, either on land or sea. When she's ashore she looks at the ocean, and when she's swimming she puts her head up and looks at you—have you seen it?—as if she wants to come up on land again."

"I know someone…a woman back home…just like that."

"They're some who are like that, they can't help it, poor

souls," Mrs. Corley nodded. "But have you ever heard the story of the Selkie Wife?"

I shook my head.

"Selkie, that's an old Gaelic word for the seal. Selchie. Silkie. All those words are the same one. So, then, there's a story that a man found a beautiful woman sleeping on the shore, without her clothes if you can believe it. He watched her that day and others, and saw how she slipped in and out of the sealskin she had nearby to her. And he determined to steal that skin so she could never more swim away. He wanted to have her for his wife, do you see? And he did take the skin and hid it away, and she did become his wife.

"He brought her home, and she gave him one child and then two more, and was always a good wife to him. But never was she completely happy, never was she at ease. Always walking by the shore, she was, and staring out. And from time to time she tore the house apart looking for that skin of hers.

"And her children knew that she was looking for something, and one day her little boy found it hidden away where his father had put it, and he gave it to her.

"And she was off. From one day to the next, gone."

I thought of you when I heard this story; but mostly I thought of Diana. Diana who had married young and had had a child so soon, only to decide, when Tracy was just six months old, that she had to leave her husband and find herself, her lesbian self.

Diana was ten years younger than me. She'd never had a job she really liked, had never held one for more than a year. She wasn't yet 30, and yet she was convinced that life had passed her by. All the time I'd known her she had worried and complained about this, but in the last years it had come up again and again.

"I never had a chance to really live, to experiment, to be young, to be a young *dyke,*" she said. "I dropped out of college to have Tracy and ever since then I've been somehow gasping for air. My head is just above water, my eyes never seem to clear enough to let me see what I really want."

I thought that I could make everything right for her. For both of them.

"You're so stable," Diana would say to me the first year. "What can you possibly see in me?"

A woman that I loved right from the start. With a daughter I could delight in and raise as my own.

"It's not fair," Diana used to joke. "How can I compare you with anyone? *You've* had half a dozen girlfriends before me. I've never had anyone but you."

"Sex is always the same, in the end," I told her, lying. "But love hardly ever comes along."

But in the end she wept. "I feel so trapped by life, by Tracy, by you. You know what you want. I've never known."

I never wanted to possess you, Silkie. I could have taken your knapsack, could have brought you back to Mrs. Corley's and made you my wife. Or just my new roommate.

Mrs. Corley wouldn't have minded. "Seals used to be human," she had ended her story. "Or maybe it was the other way around. Then we were separated, and one of us began to kill the other."

I could have tried to hold on to you, after you pressed me

to your warm damp body and took me where you took me, to some lush wet dark kingdom bannered and splintered with light. But you always left me on the shore, not satiated but complete, and I let go of you and slept and woke refreshed and quiet.

Even when it rained, even when the weather turned wilder and rainier in late September, I went looking for you. I stood on the shore and called your name.

You answered and you came. You took me in your arms and enveloped me, so that the salt water was no longer bitter on my lips or stung my eyes. Until I had no more longing for what had been or might have been, but was content and was complete.

I called Diana a few days ago. Since then I have been looking for you every morning and haven't found you. This morning I went earlier, hoped to find you sleeping with your knapsack a few feet away. Imagined sitting on your sealskin and capturing you.

I can understand why you would stay away.

Two weeks ago I wrote to Tracy, a long letter all about the travels that brought me to the Irish coast. Back came another letter from her, large-lettered and urgent. "When are you coming back?" she wrote, and then, "We MISS you."

I called Diana. She was hesitant. Things were pretty good, she said. They had roommates in the house to make the mortgage. "A couple," she said. "I watch them and I'm both envious and not. My life's so busy now, I don't want to be involved. I've gone back to community college. I'm going to finish my degree. I will! So I'm in school every evening."

"Diana, that's great!" I said, without another thought. "But...Tracy?"

"Baby-sitters, or Helen and Tina keep an eye out for her. It's not the best, but..."

I wanted to say, "Let me come back. I'll take care of her every night." My heart broke to think of my Tracy all alone.

"She misses you something terrible," Diana said. "I'm just not the same, even when I am home. It was a world you shared, books, games, magic things I didn't even know about. I always thought it was because you worked in the schools, were a librarian, that you had some special way with kids. You know," she paused and sighed, "I was always a little jealous of you. The fun you could have with Tracy while I sat and stewed about all the things in life I was losing out on."

A pause. Then, low, she asked, "When will you...will you...?"

I won't deny that it was tempting. To say, "I'm coming home. Let me back in your life again."

"There's someone else," I said instead.

"I thought so." She was strong. "It's why you didn't come back in September, isn't it?"

"Yes."

"Tracy will be so disappointed."

"Tell her that I'm happy. And I'll write to her every week and tell her stories like I used to. And I won't be gone forever. Only for a while. Till this is over."

"It's ironic," said Diana. "I thought I was leaving you, for a brave new life. And you're the one who found a new lover."

"You do have a brave new life. And I'm proud of you."

When I hung up the phone, Mrs. Corley was nearby, offering tea. "Was that your daughter you were speaking to, then?"

"My daughter's mother," I said, as plainly as I could.

I think she understood me. She said, "Well, then, that's all right then."

I went down to the sea again this morning. Called your name. There was no answer from the rocks. The waves dashed cold at my feet. I could not imagine going in the water by myself to look for you. For I would surely drown. Perhaps you'd said good-bye the last time and I hadn't heard you. Perhaps you knew that I had it in my heart to leave you eventually and return home, and wanted it to be now, rather than later.

I came in windblown and Mrs. Corley didn't ask me where I'd been. I ate my breakfast, went to the parlor and began to write a long letter to Tracy. It was about Ireland and the seals.

I told her the story of the Selkie Wife.

Late this afternoon, I read it to Mrs. Corley, asked her if I had the details right.

"Now I see why you are always reading those children's books," she said. "You're going to write one of your own, and here's your first."

"No, it's a letter to my daughter, to Tracy," I said. "I just wrote down the story that you told me."

"But I never told you about the water being veils and how the rocks felt when the seal came up on land. You wrote that all yourself."

I was taken aback. I had.

"And you never wanted to be a writer?" she asked.

"Well, yes. Once. But I never thought I could. So I went to library school and got a good job and was happy there."

The past tense had slipped out. I added, determined to be truthful, "I lost my job last spring."

"Then you're lucky," she said. "For now you've found a new one, and it suits you."

I took a nap soon after that and slept as soundly as I ever had and dreamed of you. You were in your sealskin, but with your human eyes, and we were in the water together. For the first time you did not hold me and I did not hold on to you. We swam alongside each other, me with my arms and legs and you with your fins. We swam a long time in the shallow water and then the deep, and then you led me back to shore. We raised our heads above the water and stared full in each other's eyes. We made a cry that could have been a long lament; it could have been a peal of joy.

For everything that we had lost.

For all that we'd been given.

Notes on the Retold Stories

"Wood" is based on the Grimms' fairy tale "Frau Trude."

"The Woman Who Married Her Son's Wife" is from the Eskimo tale of the same name, collected by Angela Carter in *The Old Wives' Fairy Tale Book.*

"Suit of Leather" comes from the Egyptian fairy tale "The Princess in the Suit of Leather," collected by Angela Carter in *The Old Wives' Fairy Tale Book.* It is a common European tale as well, under the name "Donkeyskins."

"Silkie" is based on the Selkie legend of the Gaelic peoples of Scotland and Ireland.